…ach
…ves in
…otte, Olivia and
…en, and continue to be, the
greatest inspirations in her life.

THE ITALIAN'S ONE-NIGHT CONSEQUENCE

CATHY WILLIAMS

MILLS & BOON

First Published in Great Britain 2018
by Mills & Boon, an imprint of HarperCollins*Publishers*
1 London Bridge Street, London, SE1 9GF

© 2018 Cathy Williams

ISBN: 978-0-263-93466-3

MIX
Paper from
responsible sources
FSC™ C007454

This book is produced from independently certified FSC™ paper
to ensure responsible forest management.
For more information visit www.harpercollins.co.uk/green.

Printed and bound in Spain
by CPI, Barcelona

CHAPTER ONE

FROM THE BACK seat of his chauffeur-driven car, which was parked a discreet distance away, Leo Conti took a few minutes to savour the edifice that dominated this tree-lined Dublin road. Prime location, perfect size, and with all the discernible signs of wear and tear that indicated a department store clinging to life by the skin of its teeth.

Frankly, things couldn't have been better.

This was the store his grandfather had spent a lifetime trying to acquire. It was the store that had eluded the old man's grasp for over fifty years, always just out of reach. Despite the vast property portfolio Benito Conti had built up over the decades, and the grand shopping complexes he had opened across the globe, this one department store had continued to hold sway over him.

Leo, raised by his grandparents from the age of eight, had never been able to understand why his grandfather couldn't just let it go—but then, being outmanoeuvred by someone you'd once considered your closest friend would leave a sour taste in anybody's mouth.

Which said something about the nature of trust.

Over the years Leo had witnessed his grandfather's

frustrated attempts to purchase the department store from Tommaso Gallo to no avail.

'He would rather it crumble to the ground,' Benito had grumbled, 'than sell it to me. Too damn proud! Well, if it *does* crumble—and crumble it will, because Tommaso has been drinking and gambling his money away for decades—I will be the first in line to laugh! The man has no honour.'

Honour, Leo thought now, as his sharp eyes continued to take in the outward signs of decay, was an irrational emotion that always led to unnecessary complications.

'Find yourself something to do, James,' Leo said to his chauffeur, leaning forward, eyes still on the building. 'Buy yourself a decent meal somewhere. Take a break from that fast food junk you insist on eating. I'll call you when it's time for you to swing by and collect me.'

'You plan on buying the place today, boss?'

A shadow of a smile crossed Leo's face. He caught his driver's eyes in the rearview mirror. James Cure— driver, dogsbody and rehabilitated petty thief—was one of the few people Leo would actually trust with his life.

'I plan,' Leo drawled, opening the passenger door and letting in a blast of summer heat, 'on having a little incognito tour to find out just how low I can go when it comes to putting money on the table. From what I see, the old man has died leaving a nice, healthy liability behind, and from what I understand, the new owner—whoever he is—will want to sell before the dreaded words *fire sale* start circulating in the business community.'

Leo had no idea who the new owner was. In fact he wouldn't have known that Tommaso Gallo had gone to meet his maker a mere month previously if his grandfather hadn't summoned him back from Hong Kong to buy the store before it went to someone else.

'Now,' Leo said, briskly winding up the conversation, 'off you go, James—and while you're finding yourself a nice, healthy salad for lunch, try and locate the nearest pawn shop, so that you can offload that array of jewellery you insist on wearing.' Leo grinned. 'Hasn't anyone told you that medallions, signet rings and thick gold chains are things of the past?'

James smiled and rolled his eyes before driving off.

Still grinning from the familiar exchange, Leo strolled towards the bank of revolving glass doors, joining the very small number of shoppers coming and going—which, on what should have been a busy Saturday morning in the height of summer, pretty much said it all about the state of the department store.

Four storeys of glass and concrete, heading for the knacker's yard. Mentally he dropped the price he'd had in his head by a couple of hundred thousand.

His grandfather, he thought wryly, would be pleased as Punch. He would have found it galling to have paid top whack for a place he privately thought should have belonged to him fifty years ago, had Tommaso Gallo been prepared to honour the deal he had promised.

Strolling away from the revolving doors towards the store guide by the escalator, Leo gave some thought to the tales about the now legendary feud that had been part and parcel of life as he had grown up.

Two friends—both from Italy, both talented, both seeking to make their fortunes in Ireland. One small, dilapidated shop, up for sale at a knockdown price. But sitting on a slice of street that both Tommaso and Benito had fast recognised would be worth a lot in years to come. The drift of business hadn't quite reached that part of the city then, but it would.

They could have done the sensible thing and gone into business together, but instead they had tossed a coin after way too many drinks. Winner to take all. A drunken handshake had sealed the bet that would prove the unravelling of their friendship—for Benito had won the toss, fair and square, only for his one-time friend to go behind his back and snap up the property before Benito had been able to get his finances together.

Bitter, Benito had retreated to London where, over time, he had made his own vast fortune—but he had never forgiven Tommaso for his treachery. Nor had he ever stopped wanting that one department store, which he really didn't need because he had quite enough of his own.

Leo knew that he could have worked a little harder to dampen his grandfather's desire to have something that no longer mattered, all things considered, but he loved his grandfather and, much as he didn't believe in emotions overriding common sense, he had to admit that something in him could understand the need for some sort of retribution after such an act of betrayal.

And also, from a practical point of view, it would certainly work in Leo's interests to have the place. Dublin would be an excellent addition to his own massive portfolio of companies. He had already agreed with his grandfather that once the store was back in Conti hands he, Leo, would do with it as he wished, with the proviso that the name Conti replaced Gallo.

Leo had argued with his grandfather, wanting him to allow him to pay for the purchase himself. Because there was no way he intended to leave it as a cumbersome department store, however iconic it had once been.

That sort of sentimentality wasn't for him. No, Leo wanted the place because he liked the thought of finally getting his foot into Dublin—something long denied him because he had never found the perfect property to set down roots.

Along with his own start-up companies Leo had acquired a string of software and IT companies, which he had merged under one umbrella and continued to run while simultaneously overseeing Benito's empire by proxy. He had only a handful of outlets for his highly specialised merchandise, where expert advice was on hand for the elite group of medical, architectural and engineering giants who used what he had to offer.

This site would be perfect for expanding his businesses into a new market.

His thoughts far away, he was already indulging in the pleasurable exercise of planning how he would use the space to its best advantage.

Naturally it would have to be gutted. Wood, carpet and dowdy furnishings might have worked back in the day—although to be fair Leo wasn't sure *when* that day might have been—but as soon as he got his hands on the store they'd have to go. God knew, the place was probably riddled with rising damp, dry rot and termites. By the time he was through with it, and the 'Gallo' sign had been unceremoniously dumped, it would be unrecognisable.

He looked around, wondering which decrepit part of the store he should hit first—and there she was.

Standing behind one of the make-up counters, she looked as out of place as a fish in a bookstore. Despite the fact that she was surrounded by all manner of war paint, in expensive jars and shiny compact holders, she herself appeared to be devoid of any cosmetics. Frowning at an arrangement of dark burgundy pots on the glass counter, and needlessly repositioning them, she was the very picture of natural, stunningly beautiful freshness, and for a few seconds Leo actually held his breath as he stared at her.

His libido, which had been untested for the past three weeks, ever since he had broken up with his latest conquest after she'd started making unfortunate noises about permanence and commitment, sprang into enthusiastic life.

Leo was so surprised at his reaction that he was hardly aware that he was staring like a horny teenager. Not cool. Not *him*.

Especially when the leggy girl he was staring at was definitely *not* a Page Three girl and even more definitely *not* the sort of woman he was attracted to.

She was tall and willowy, from the little he could make out under the cheap store uniform, and she had the sort of wide-eyed innocence that was always accompanied in his head with the strident ringing of alarm bells. Her skin was smooth and satiny and the colour of pale caramel, as though she had been toasted in the sun. Her hair was tied back, but the bits escaping were a shade darker than her skin, toffee-coloured with strands of strawberry blonde running through it.

And her eyes…

She abruptly stopped what she was doing and looked up, gazing directly back at him.

Her eyes were green—as clear as glass washed up on a beach.

The kick of sexual attraction, a lust as raw as any-thing he'd ever felt before, shot through him like a bolt of adrenaline, and Leo felt himself harden in immedi-ate response. It was fierce enough to take his mind off everything that had hitherto been occupying it.

His stiffened shaft was painful, and he had to adjust his position to release some of the pressure. As their eyes tangled he thought that if she kept looking at him like that, making him imagine what it would be like to have that succulent full mouth circling the throbbing, rigid length of him, he would soon be desperate for release.

He began walking towards her, every hunting in-stinct inside him honing in on his prey. He'd never wanted any woman with such urgent immediacy be-fore and Leo wasn't about to ignore the pull. When it came to sex, he was a man who had always got what he wanted—and he wanted this woman with every fibre in his body.

The closer he got to her, the more stupendously pretty she was. Her huge eyes were almond-shaped, fringed with very dark lashes that seemed to contradict the colour of her hair. Her lips, parted, were sensuous and full, even though their startled-in-the-headlights expression was teasingly innocent. And her body...

The unappealing, clinical white dress, belted at the waist, should have been enough to dampen any man's ardour, but instead it sent his imagination into frantic overdrive and he caught himself wondering what her breasts would look like, what they would taste like...

'Can I help you?' Maddie's heart was beating like a sledgehammer, but her expression was studiously po-lite as she met the stranger's openly appreciative gaze.

Man sees girl. Man is attracted to girl. Man makes beeline for girl because he has one thing on his mind and that's getting her into bed with him.

Maddie was used to that response from the opposite sex. She hated it.

What was even more galling was the fact that this particular man had, just for a second, aroused something in her *other* than her usual instinct to slam down the shutters hard the minute she saw a come-on situation on the horizon.

In fact, for a second, she had felt a stirring between her thighs—a tingling, tickly *melting* that had horrified her.

'Interesting question,' the man murmured, positioning himself directly in front of her.

The look in her eyes seemed to amuse him.

'Are you looking for make-up?' Maddie asked bluntly. 'Because if so you're in the wrong department. I could always point you in the right direction.'

In response, the man randomly picked up a jar from the precarious display she had been fiddling with earlier and twirled it in his hand.

'What's this if not make-up?'

Maddie removed it from him and swivelled it so that the label was facing him. 'Regenerating night cream, targeting a woman in her sixties,' she said crisply. 'Are you interested in buying it?'

'Oh, I'm *interested*,' he said, in a tone laced with innuendo.

'Well, that's all I'm selling, so if it's not what you're *interested* in you should probably keep moving.'

Maddie folded her arms. She knew she was blushing. She also knew that her body was misbehaving. Once upon a time, it had misbehaved before, and she still had the scars to show for that. A repeat performance wasn't on the cards—especially not with some arrogant guy too good-looking for his own good.

'Are we cutting to the chase, here?' Leo purred, rising to the challenge and liking it. 'Who's to say I'm not...*interested*...in that very expensive pot of cream for my mother?'

'Oh!' Maddie flushed. She'd misread the situation.

At this rate, sampling how things worked on the shop floor was going to get her precisely nowhere—because she clearly had no idea about effective salesmanship. But then she'd never stood behind a counter selling anything in her entire life.

Yet again she wondered whether she was doing the right thing. *Was* she? Three and a half weeks ago she'd received the startling news that she was the sole beneficiary of a bequest that included a department store, a house, and various assorted paraphernalia—courtesy of a grandfather she had never seen, nor met, and never really known existed.

Having been struggling to make ends meet, and living the sort of disastrous life she had never imagined possible, she had already been asking herself what direction she needed to take to wipe away the past couple of years of her life, or at least to put it all in perspective, and *wham*—just like that, she'd received her answer.

She'd arrived in Ireland still barely able to believe her good fortune, with big plans to sell the store, the house and whatever else there was to sell, so that she could buy herself the dream that had eluded her for so many years.

An education.

With money in the bank she would be able to get to university, an ambition she had had to abandon when her mother had become ill four years previously. She would be able to throw herself into the art course she had always wanted to do without fear of finding herself begging on street corners to pay for the privilege.

She would be able to *make* something of herself—and that meant a lot, because she felt that she'd spent much of her life being buffeted by the winds of fate, carried this way and that with no discernible goal propelling her forward.

But she'd taken one look at the store and one look at the house she had inherited—full of charm despite the fact that it was practically falling down—and she'd dumped all her plans to sell faster than a rocket leaving earth. Art school could wait—the store needed her love and her help *now*.

Anthony Grey, the lawyer who had arranged to see her so that he could go over every single disadvantage of hanging on to what, apparently, was a business on its last legs and a house that was being propped up only by the ivy growing around it, had talked to her for three hours. She had listened with her head tilted to one side, hands on her knees, and had then promptly informed him that she was going to try and make a go of it.

And that, first and foremost, entailed getting to know what it was she intended making a go of. Which, in turn, necessitated her working on the shop floor so that she could see where the cracks were and also hopefully pick up what was being said by the loyal staff who suspected that their jobs might be hanging in the balance.

A couple of weeks under cover and Maddie was sure she would be able to get a feel for things.

Optimism hadn't been her companion for a very long time and she had been enjoying it.

Until now. She'd jumped to all sorts of conclusions and screwed up. She pinned a smile to her face, because the way too good-looking man staring down at her, with the most incredible navy blue eyes she had ever seen in her life, looked rich and influential, even though he was kitted out in a pair of faded black jeans and a polo shirt.

There was something about his lazy, loose-limbed stance, the way he oozed self-confidence, the latent strength of his body...

She felt it again—that treacherous quiver in the pit of her stomach and the tickling between her thighs—and she furiously stamped it down.

'Your mother...' She picked up the pot and squinted at it. 'She'd love this. It's thick, creamy, and excellent at smoothing out wrinkles.'

'Are you just reading what's written on the label?'

'I'm afraid I've only been here a short while, so I'm just getting the hang of things.'

'Shouldn't you have a supervisor working with you in that case? Showing you the ropes?'

The man looked around, as though expecting said person to materialise in front of him. He was *enjoying* himself. It was clear this stranger was so accustomed to women fawning over him that the novel experience of a woman not caring who he was or how much he was worth was tickling him pink.

He rested flattened palms on the glass counter and Maddie shifted back just a little.

'Dereliction of duty,' he murmured.

'I beg your pardon?'

'You need to tell your boss that it gives the customer a poor impression if the people working on the sales floor don't really know what they're talking about.'

Maddie stiffened at the criticism. 'You'll find that everyone else on the shop floor has worked here for a very long time. If you like, I can fetch someone over here to help you in your…your quest for the perfect face cream for your mother.'

'I'll let you in on a little secret,' the man said with a tinge of regret, his navy blue eyes never once leaving her face. 'I lied about wanting the cream for my mother. My mother died when I was a boy.' Sincere regret seeped into his voice. 'Both my parents, in actual fact,' he added in a roughened undertone.

'I'm so sorry.'

Maddie still felt the loss of her own mother, but she had had her around for a great deal longer than the man standing in front of her had had his. Her father had never been in the picture. He'd done a runner before she was old enough to walk.

Maddie knew scraps of the story that had brought her mother from Italy to the other side of the world. There had been an argument between her mother and the grandfather Maddie hadn't ever known which had never been resolved. Harsh words exchanged and then too much pride on both sides for any resolution until time took over, making reconciliation an impossibility.

Her mother had been a strong woman—someone who had planted both feet and stood her ground. Stubborn… But then she'd had to fight her way in Australia with a young baby to take care of. Maddie felt that her grandfather might have had the same traits—although she had no real idea because she'd never been told. Secretly she wondered if the grandfather she'd never met might have attempted to contact her mother, only to have his efforts spurned. Parents were often more forgiving with their children than the other way around.

Her eyes misted over and she reached out and impulsively circled the man's wrist with her fingers— and then yanked her hand back because the charge of electricity that shot through her was downright frightening.

He raised his eyebrows, and for a second she felt that he could read every thought that had flashed through her head.

'No need,' he murmured. 'Have dinner with me.'

'I beg your pardon?'

'I'll pass on the face cream. Frankly, all those wild claims can't possibly be true. But have dinner with me. Name the place, name the time…'

'You're not interested in buying anything in this store, are you?'

Maddie's voice cooled by several degrees, because he was just another example of a cocky guy who wanted to get her into bed. She'd been spot-on first time round.

'And as for a dinner date… That'll be a *no*.'

Dinner with this man? How arrogant was he?

Her eyes slid surreptitiously over him and she understood very well why he was as arrogant as he was. The guy was drop-dead gorgeous.

Lean, perfectly chiselled features, dark hair worn slightly too long, which emphasised his powerful masculinity rather than detracting from it, a tightly honed body that testified to time spent working out, even though he didn't look like the sort of man who spent much time preening in front of mirrors and flexing his muscles. And those eyes… Sexy, bedroom eyes that made her skin burn and made her thoughts wander to what a dinner date with him might be like…

She forced herself to conjure up the hateful memory of her ex—Adam. He'd been good-looking too. Plus charming, charismatic, and from the sort of family that had spent generations looking down on people like her. Well, that whole experience had been a learning curve for Maddie, and she wasn't about to put those valuable lessons to waste by succumbing to the phoney charm of the man in front of her with his sinful good looks and his *I could make your body sing* bedroom eyes.

'Should I be?'

Maddie frowned. 'What do you mean? What are you talking about?'

'*Should* I be interested in buying anything here? Look around you. This is a department store that's gone to rack and ruin. I'm staggered that you would even have contemplated working here in the first place. The job situation in Dublin must be dire for you to have settled on *this*—and you've obviously had no on-the-job training because there isn't enough money to go round for such essentials as training programmes. I'm pretty sure that if I looked I'd find an array of out-of-date merchandise and demotivated sales assistants.'

'Who *are* you?'

Maddie looked at him narrowly. Was she missing something?

Leo met her stare and held it. He'd planned on a little incognito surveillance and he was going to stick to the plan—bar this little detour which, he thought, he could very well use to his advantage. She'd turned down his dinner date but he wasn't fazed by that. Women never said no to him for very long.

Although…

He frowned, because *this* particular woman didn't seem to fit the mould.

'Just someone browsing,' Leo said smoothly, and then he added, truthfully, 'I don't get to this part of the world very often and I wanted to see this store everyone seems to know about.' He looked around him. 'I'm less than impressed.'

The woman followed his gaze and said nothing, perhaps because she'd noticed those very same signs of disrepair. She seemed to suddenly realise that he was still watching her, his eyes narrowed.

'I can see that you agree with me.'

'Like I said, I haven't been here for very long—but if you're looking for something to buy as a souvenir of the store, there's an excellent selection on the second floor. Mugs, tote bags, lots of stuff…'

Leo suppressed a shudder at the image of tackiness created in his head. Had the place moved with the times *at all*? Or had progress being quietly sidelined as Gallo's money ran out?

He had a satisfying vision of what the place would look like under his dominion. High-tech, white glossy counters and open, uncluttered spaces, glass and mirrors, ranks of computers and accessories waiting to be explored—no irritating background elevator music and salespeople who actually knew what they were talking about.

'If you have lots of money to spend, then we offer a range of leather handbags which we manufacture ourselves to the highest possible standard. They're Italian, and really beautiful quality.'

'Sadly,' Leo said, easily giving voice to the lie, 'my finances would struggle to stretch to one of your leather handbags.'

She nodded. He didn't seem like the sort of broke, wrong-side-of-the-tracks kind of guy she had encountered during her life, but it was a fact that a good-looking man could look expensive in anything.

'But I could probably stretch to one of those tote things you mentioned...'

'Second floor.'

'Take me.'

'Come again?'

'I want you to do your sales pitch on me.'

'I'll be honest with you,' she said flatly, 'if this is another way of trying to get me to have dinner with you, then you can forget it. I won't be doing that.'

Leo wondered whether she would have had a change of heart had she known his true worth. Most definitely, he thought, with his usual healthy dose of cynicism. That said, he was a man accustomed to getting what he wanted—and the more he talked to her, looked at her, felt the pleasurable race of his pulses and the hard throb of his libido, the more he wanted to rise to the challenge of breaking down whatever walls she felt she had to erect.

For once, work and the reason he was in this sad excuse of a store had been put on the back burner.

'You're very arrogant, aren't you?' he murmured, watching her carefully as the slow burn of anger turned her cheeks a healthy pink. 'Do you think that you have what it takes to make a man keep banging on a door that's been firmly shut in his face?'

'How *dare* you?'

'You forget—I'm the customer and the customer is always right.'

His grin was meant to take the sting out of his words and make her realise that he'd been teasing her.

'That's better,' Leo said as her anger appeared to fade, then glanced at his watch to find that time had flown by. 'Now, why don't you show me this souvenir section of yours?' He raised both hands in mock surrender. 'And you can breathe safe in the knowledge that there'll be no more dinner invitations. You say you're new here… You can practise your sales patter on me. I'm just passing through, so you won't have to worry that I'll be gossiping behind your back with the locals, telling them that the new girl at the big store doesn't seem to know the ropes.'

Maddie looked down, but she wanted to smile.

So far she'd made no friends. It would take time for her to integrate. This interaction almost felt like a breath of fresh air. Naturally she wasn't going to be an idiot and go on any dates with any strangers—especially good-looking ones who obviously knew how to say the right things to get a woman's pulse racing. But he had valid criticisms of the store, and she would need those—would need to find out what customers thought when they entered. Customers would look at the place through different eyes from hers. It might actually be a good idea to encourage his opinions.

So he'd asked her out… Maddie didn't spend time staring at her reflection in mirrors, but she knew that she was attractive. It was something that had dogged her, for better or for worse. Certainly for worse when it had come to Adam, but she couldn't let the memory of that determine every single response to every single guy who happened to look in her direction. Could she?

Besides, setting aside the killer looks, the man still staring at her wasn't a rich creep—like Adam had been, had she only had the wisdom to see that from the very start. This guy was more tote bags than soft Italian leather.

Maddie felt a thrilling little frisson as she breathed in deeply and said, 'Well, I guess I could get someone to cover for me just for a little while.'

Brian Walsh was in charge of the store temporarily, and he was the only one who knew who she really was. He had worked there for over twenty years and was keen to see the store become again the place it had once been, so he was fully on board with her decision to evaluate the store undercover for a short period of time while she worked out a way forward.

'My…er…my boss is just over there. I'll ask his… er…permission…'

'Your boss?' he asked, his interest clearly pricked by the knowledge.

'Mr Walsh. If you don't mind waiting…?'

'I have all the time in the world,' he said expansively, deciding on the spot to tell James to head back to the hotel, just in case he found himself staying longer than anticipated. 'I'll be right here when you return.'

CHAPTER TWO

LEO COULD HAVE taken the opportunity to probe her about her boss—the man Leo would soon be putting through the wringer—but that, he decided as he watched her heading back towards him, could wait. His grandfather wanted the store *yesterday*, but tomorrow or the day after was just fine with Leo. There was no doubt in his mind that he would secure the store—so what was the harm in letting himself be temporarily distracted?

She moved like a dancer, her body erect, looking neither right nor left as she walked gracefully across the department store floor. He suddenly realised he didn't even know her name, and he put that right the minute she was standing in front of him again, her fresh, floral scent filling his nostrils and turning him on.

'Shouldn't you be wearing a name tag? Something discreetly pinned to your nice white outfit so that I know exactly who to complain about if you sell me overpriced face cream that makes my girlfriend's skin break out in spots?'

'You have a girlfriend?'

The interest in her voice pleased him.

'Because,' she went on quickly, the flush on her cheeks betraying the fact that she'd realised her slip, 'if you do, then you should have said. I could have pointed you in the direction of a whole different selection of face products.'

Leo glanced down at her. She was tall. Much taller than the women he was fond of dating. 'Alas, that's a position that's waiting to be filled,' he murmured. 'And it has to be said that, as presents go, anti-wrinkle, anti-ageing face cream wouldn't make a good one for any of the women I've ever dated in the past. So, what *is* your name?'

'Madison.' She kept her eyes professionally forward as the escalator took them up one floor and then the next, up to the second floor, where any visible effort at revitalisation had been abandoned. Here, the décor begged to be revamped and the displays craved some sort of creative, modern overhaul.

'Madison…?'

'But everyone calls me Maddie. We're here.'

She began walking towards the back of the floor while Leo took his time strolling slightly behind her, taking in the store's rundown appearance. He was surprised spiders weren't weaving cobwebs between the dated merchandise—although he had to concede the sales assistants they passed were all wearing cheerful smiles.

Attention distracted, he glanced at the arrangement of souvenirs, all bearing the Gallo logo. Absently he toyed with a canvas bag, and then he looked at her seriously.

'You're not Irish.' He dropped the bag and it dangled forlornly on its rack.

'No. Well, not exactly.'

Maddie looked at him and felt her insides swoop.

Even standing at a respectable distance away from her, he still seemed to invade her personal space. He was so…*big*…and his presence was so…*suffocatingly powerful*. Curiosity gripped her, and she wondered who exactly he was and what he did.

Where did he live? Why would a man like this be dawdling on a Saturday morning in this particular department store?

Alarmed, she cleared her throat, but for some reason found herself unable to drag her eyes away from his stunningly beautiful face. 'Australia. I'm Australian.'

'You've come from the other side of the world to work *here*?'

'Are you always so…so *rude*… Mr…? I don't even know your name!'

'You mean just in case you want to complain about me to your boss? My name is Leo. Shall we shake hands and make the introductions formal?'

Maddie stuck her hands firmly behind her back and glowered. 'I feel I can speak on behalf of my boss when I say that it's always useful to hear constructive criticism about the store, but your criticism isn't at all constructive, Mr… Mr…'

'Leo.'

She glanced around her and winced slightly at what she saw. 'I believe,' she said carefully, 'that the owner of the store passed away a short time ago. I don't think much has been done in terms of modernisation in recent years.'

'I have some experience of the retail market,' Leo said absently, his eyes still wandering over the shelves and wares around them.

Suddenly those eyes were back on hers and a smile tugged at his lips.

'This isn't a dinner invitation, but I see that there's a coffee shop on this floor. If you'd find it helpful, I could give you a few pearls of wisdom...'

'You've run a department store in the past?'

Leo grinned, his deep blue eyes lazy and amused. 'I wouldn't quite put it like that...'

'I get it.'

Maddie knew all about doing menial jobs to earn a living. She also knew all about the way people could look at someone attractive and misconstrue their place in the great pecking order. *She* didn't look like someone who should be mopping floors in a hospital on the outskirts of Sydney. If she had, her life would never have ended up taking the unfortunate twists and turns that it had.

She met his direct gaze and smiled.

That smile knocked Leo sideways. Just like that he wanted to drag her away from the tasteless display of goods, pull her into the nearest cupboard and get underneath that prim and proper clinical white get-up that wouldn't have gone amiss on a dental assistant. He wanted to kiss her raspberry-pink lips, crush them under his mouth, feel her tongue lashing against his, and then slowly, bit by bit, he wanted to get up close and personal with her body.

He suppressed a groan. She was still smiling, and his erection was getting more rigid by the second. He had to look away to catch his breath and focus on something innocuous. A stack of Gallo-label tea towels did the trick.

'You do?'

'I can understand. I've had lots of menial jobs in the past. Trust me—it's heavenly being here.' Maddie said it with the utmost sincerity.

Somehow they were walking away from the souvenir section towards the café.

Leo turned to her, his fingers hooking in the waistband of his low slung faded jeans.

'I'm thinking you'll probably get in trouble with the boss if you take time out to have a coffee with me.'

'I expect I might.'

The fierce antagonism that had filled her when she'd thought he was after her seemed to have evaporated. Somehow he'd managed to put her at ease. And Maddie wasn't sure whether to be alarmed at that development or happy about it.

Ever since Adam she'd made a habit of practically crossing the road to the other side of the street every time she spotted a man heading in her direction. Events had conspired to turn her social life, sparse as it had been, into a no-go zone. Men had been the first casualty of her experience with Adam and friends had fast followed, because her trust had been broken down to the point where it had all but disappeared.

But should she allow those experiences to follow her all the way to the other side of the world?

This was going to be her new home, and the last thing she wanted to do was to commence life in her new home as a crazy lady recluse.

Yes, warning bells had sounded when she'd first met Leo. But he wasn't rich, and as soon as she'd told him to back off he'd backed off. He wasn't from the area. He wasn't going to be around. He was also happy to talk to her about the store, and she could use a little impartial advice—even though he wouldn't know the reasons behind her wanting to hear what he had to say.

Sometimes nomads and wanderers—people who fell in and out of jobs— picked up life lessons along the way, and the very fact that they were streetwise gave them an added insight into life. Taking the path of adventure, untethered by the ropes that held most people down, brought its own rewards.

And, my word, was the man sexy...

She looked at him, every nerve-ending in her body tingling as he settled his fabulous eyes on her and allowed the silence between them to stretch to breaking point.

'How long are you going to be in this lovely city?' Maddie asked a little breathlessly, and Leo shrugged.

'Perhaps not even overnight,' he mused, harking back to his original plan and marvelling at the speed with which it had changed course along the way. Just as well as he was a man who could think on his feet and adapt.

At any rate, he'd probably seen everything there was to see with regard to the condition of the store, short of tapping on walls and peering into cupboards. He knew enough to settle the thorny matter of how much he should offer for the place and how fast he should move. He presumed the boss was ready to throw the towel in.

But that wasn't what was putting a smile on his face at the moment.

'It might be nice to…er…to have dinner with you.' Maddie blushed and glanced away.

'May I ask what's prompted the change of heart?' Leo asked wryly. 'Five minutes ago I was the devil incarnate for suggesting any such thing.'

'I…' Maddie took a deep breath. 'I haven't been in

Ireland long, and it would be…nice to have some company for a couple of hours. I've more or less stayed in on my own for the past few weeks.'

With her looks, Leo mused, solitude would have to be her chosen option—because she'd only have to step foot out of her front door and company would be available in any direction she chose to look.

But then that probably wasn't the sort of company she had in mind. The sort of company that came with strings attached. The sort of company she had assumed *he'd* been offering—and, frankly, her assumptions had been dead-on.

Leo wasn't surprised that her looks had made her wary of the attention she got—had made her guarded and cynical about what men wanted from her. It wasn't that different from the way his vast wealth had made *him* guarded and cynical when it came to the opposite sex.

He wasn't looking for commitment and he didn't do declarations of love. He enjoyed impermanence when it came to women.

Leo didn't know whether he might have gone down the normal route of marriage, two point two kids and a house in the country—or in his case several houses in several countries—if bitter experience hadn't taught him the value of steering clear of relationships.

His grandparents had been very happily married. His parents, he had been told, had likewise been very happily married—indeed, had been on something of a second honeymoon when a lorry, going too fast in bad weather, had slammed into their little Fiat and crushed it.

He had not been blighted by poor childhood memories or affected by warring parents or evil stepmothers. Alcohol, drug abuse and infidelity had been conspicuously and thankfully absent from his life. *His* cautionary tales stemmed from an altogether different source.

He shrugged aside this lapse in concentration as well as any niggling of his conscience, by reminding himself that he was as honourable as they came, because he was always, *always* upfront in his relationships. He told it like it was.

Sex and fun, but no cosy nights in front of the telly, no meeting the parents.

That said, he was a one-woman man, and any woman he dated would have all of him—if only for a limited amount of time. Largely, he was the one who usually called it a day, but he was perfectly happy if it were the other way around. He was the least possessive man he knew and he liked it that way.

He looked at Maddie in silence for a little while. She'd rebuffed him first time around, and he was sharp enough to pick up that little comment about how it would *'be nice to have company for a couple of hours'*.

'Tell me where you live,' he drawled. 'I'll pick you up.'

'You have a car?'

'I have a fleet of them,' he said, which was the absolute truth. 'Of course they're garaged in London—which is where, incidentally, I have my penthouse apartment—but if you tell me which make you'd prefer, I'll make sure it's delivered to me in time to collect you later. So, what's it to be? Ferrari? Range Rover? BMW? Or maybe something classic like an Aston Martin…?'

Maddie burst out laughing. The guy had a sense of humour and she liked that. She hadn't laughed for a long time, but now she was laughing so hard that tears came to her eyes.

Finally, sobering up, she said, still smiling, 'I'll meet you somewhere. I think there are some cheap and cheerful restaurants we could go to…'

'I'll give you my number. Text me. I'll meet you there at…what? Seven? What time does this place close?'

'Seven would be great. Now, really, I have to go…'

'One last thing…' Leo looked at her seriously. 'You need not fear that I'll make a pest of myself. I won't.'

Maddie reddened and an errant thought flashed through her head,

What would it be like if you were to make a pest of yourself…?

'Good,' she said nonchalantly. 'Because I've a lot going on in my life at the moment and the last thing I need is…is…'

'Fending off a nuisance?'

'I was going to say that the last thing I need is a relationship.'

At which Leo was the one to burst out laughing. He looked at her with his midnight-blue eyes, 'Trust me—relationships don't ever feature on my agenda. See you later, Maddie.'

And he was gone, leaving her standing as still as a statue, even though inside her everything was weirdly mushy, as though she'd just stepped off a death-defying rollercoaster ride and was struggling to get her bearings.

She spent the remainder of the day in a state of low-level excitement. She told herself that this wasn't a date. Not really. This was dinner with someone who'd made her laugh—because the alternative was yet another night in, going through the mountains of paperwork her solicitor had left for her, trying to work out the best approach to take when she went to see the bank manager for a loan the following week.

She was twenty-four years old! Where was the harm in acting her age? She couldn't remember the last time she'd felt young, and the tall, dark, handsome stranger had made her feel young.

And he wasn't going to be sticking around.

By seven that evening, as she stood outside the cheap Italian restaurant where they'd arranged to meet, the nerves which had abated at some point during the day were back in full swing.

She smoothed down the front of her shirt. No one could accuse her of dressing to impress. She was in a pair of ripped jeans, some flat navy ballet pumps and a tee shirt that was a little tighter than she liked and a little shorter than she might have wanted, exposing a sliver of flat brown skin. It, like the jeans, was faded and worn.

She'd had a brief flirtation with designer dressing. Adam had liked to see her in expensive gear and, much against her will, he had encouraged her into wearing clothes that he'd bought for her—expensive, slinky silk outfits and high, high designer heels.

He'd enjoyed the way everyone's heads had turned whenever she'd stalked into a room and Maddie had gone along with it, albeit reluctantly, because she'd loved him and had wanted to please him.

She'd sent the entire lot back to his flash apartment when their relationship had crashed and burned, and had promptly returned to the sorts of clothes she'd always felt comfortable in.

Leo, at least, would appreciate her choice of clothing, since they came from the same side of the tracks.

Feeling more buoyant, she pushed open the door to the trattoria and looked around, hoping she'd arrived before he had because then she could have a drink to steady her nerves, and also hoping that she hadn't, because to arrive early might suggest that she was desperate for male company. More than that—desperate for *his* company.

Nursing a drink at the very back of the restaurant, Leo had spotted her immediately. How could he not? The entire restaurant had spotted her at roughly the same time. Every male head swung round. Mouths fell open. In fairness to her, she didn't seem to notice any of this as she peered around her, squinting into the semi-lit depths of the trattoria, which was noisy, packed and uncomfortable.

In a room full of pale faces her honeyed tan stood out, as did her hair, flowing in a wavy mane over narrow shoulders almost down to her waist. Leo half stood and she walked towards him, weaving a path through the crowds until she was right in front of him.

'Been here before?' he asked, and when she shook her head he nodded and scanned the room. 'Do you think we'll be able to have a conversation or should we resign ourselves to shouting?'

'It's cheap and cheerful. And I hear that the food's good.'

She slipped into a chair and tried not to drink in his masculine beauty. She'd just about managed to convince herself that he couldn't possibly be as striking as she remembered, but he was even more so. He radiated a dynamism that made her shiver with awareness, and his exotic colouring only added to the potent appeal of his good looks.

Very quickly Maddie had a glass of wine to calm her nerves, even though common sense told her there was nothing to be nervous about.

Certainly he was sticking to the script. If his original dinner invitation had set her antennae onto red alert, actually being here with him was doing the opposite, dispelling any misgivings she might have been harbouring about his intentions.

He was charm itself. He chatted about the many countries he had visited—which made sense because he was obviously a guy who lived for the present and absorbed whatever adventures life had to offer. It was something she really admired. He was witty and insightful, and she found herself laughing out loud at some of his anecdotes, barely noticing the antipasti he had ordered for them to share.

'I envy you,' she said truthfully as plates were cleared, glasses refilled and bowls of pasta placed in front of them. 'I've never got to travel. I would have loved to, but my mum and I barely had enough to make ends meet and we would never have been able to afford it. I guess it's a lot easier when you only have yourself to consider, and I suppose you could always pick up jobs here and there to pay your way...'

'I do try and get myself an honest day's work when I'm abroad,' he said, almost uncomfortably. 'Tell me why you've run away from Australia.'

The abrupt change in the conversation caught Maddie off-guard and she stiffened—her natural response whenever she thought about her past. What would this complete stranger think were she to tell him the truth? He might be an adventurer, living off the land and shunning responsibility, but that didn't mean that he wouldn't be judgemental if she were to share her story with him.

The *whole* of her story.

Maddie found that she didn't want him to think badly of her. 'Whoever said anything about running away?' she hedged lightly, winding long strands of spaghetti around her fork and avoiding eye contact.

Leo raised his eyebrows wryly. He sat back and gave her the benefit of his full attention, which was enough to make her blush furiously.

Her glass-green eyes drifted to his forearms, strong and muscled and sprinkled with dark hair, and she wondered what it would be like to be touched by them, to have his hands roam and explore her body. Her heart picked up speed and she licked her lips, panicked by the way her body was insisting on slipping its leash and running wild.

'Well,' Leo drawled, his voice a low murmur that made the hairs on the nape of her neck stand on end, 'looking at the facts: you're on the other side of the world, without a network of fellow travelling friends, and working in a job that can't really be classed as career-building. You haven't mentioned anything about studying, so I'm thinking that's not relevant. Which leads me to think that you're running away from something. Or someone. Or both.'

Maddie laughed, but the tide of colour in her cheeks was more vibrant now. 'My mum died,' she said, twirling the stem of her wine glass and then pausing as he filled it with more wine. 'I'd spent some time looking after her. It was very unexpected. Bad luck, really. She broke her leg, and it was a very complex break, but it should have been okay.' She blinked furiously. 'Unfortunately the operation turned out to be a fiasco. She was confined to hospital for much longer than anticipated and then she needed a great deal of further surgery. Every time she felt she was back on her feet something would go wrong and back she would have to go.'

'How old were you when all this happened?'

'Just before my twentieth birthday,' Maddie admitted.

'Must have been tough.'

'Everyone goes through tough times.' She brushed off any show of sympathy because she was close enough to tears already. But she could see sympathy in the deep navy eyes resting on her and that was weird, because her very first impression of him had been of a guy who was as hard as nails.

Something about the predatory way he moved, the cool, lazy self-assurance in his eyes, the arrogant set of his features... But then being wary of the opposite sex, suspecting the worst before the worst could happen, had become a way of life for her.

'*You* must have,' she said lightly, blushing. 'Gone through rough times, I mean? Or at least had one or two hairy encounters! Isn't that part and parcel of being a nomad? A side effect of living life as an adventurer?'

Leo was enjoying the tinge of colour staining her cheeks. *Australia.* Hence the golden hue of her skin. Next to her, the other women in the restaurant seemed pale and anaemic.

He shrugged, adept as always at evading any sort of real sharing. 'Sisters? Brothers?' he asked. 'Anyone out there for you when your mother was ill?'

'Just me.' Maddie realised that somewhere along the line food had been eaten and plates cleared away. She couldn't remember when exactly that had happened. 'My mother was from here, actually...'

'Ireland?' Startled, Leo caught her eyes.

'As a matter of fact, she was.'

Maddie wondered what he would think if she told him that she was the owner of the very store he had been busy criticising only hours before. He didn't look the type to scare easily, but men could be funny when it came to women being higher up the financial pecking order than they were.

'Hence you're returning to your motherland...?'

'I thought it made sense. I wanted to get out of Australia after...after everything...'

Leo didn't say anything, but his gaze was penetrating.

The waiter had approached, asking them what they'd thought of their meal, pressing them to sample some dessert but they both politely declined, asking only for the bill.

Maddie reached into her rucksack, withdrawing a wallet and extracting notes.

'What are you doing?' he asked with a frown.

'Paying my way.' Maddie looked at him, surprised at his reaction to what she thought was perfectly obvious.

'When I go out with a woman *I* foot the bill,' Leo asserted.

She stiffened. 'Not this woman. I pay my half. That way I'm in no one's debt.'

'The price of a cheap Italian meal doesn't put you in my *debt*.' Leo tossed a handful of euros onto the silver platter—enough to cover the meal with an overly generous tip.

'Have you never met a man who knows how to treat a woman?' he asked, rising to his feet.

Maddie thought of her ex-boyfriend. Adam had *loved* paying for things for her. Flowers, chocolates, expensive meals out—but with the lavishing of gifts had come the manacles of control, the compulsion to turn her into something he wanted. And underneath all that had been his superiority—thinking that by making her into his doll he was asserting ascendancy over her, owning her.

But she'd remained the girl from the wrong side of the tracks, and sure enough that was something that couldn't be buried under gifts and presents. Inevitably she'd learned a valuable lesson in the perils of ever thinking that someone rich and well-connected could ever be anything but condescending and manipulative.

Anyway, all those wildly expensive gifts had made her feel horribly uncomfortable, and she certainly didn't like the idea of Leo or anyone else paying for her. As she had found to her cost, there was no such thing as a free lunch.

'Are you asking me if I've ever met a man who knows how to reach for his wallet and buy me pretty baubles?' She slapped a few euros on the table. The waiter was going to be very happy indeed with the extravagant tip coming his way. 'Because if that's what you're asking then, yes, I have. And it didn't work out for me. Which is why I prefer to keep things simple and pay my way.'

She stood up, and Leo shrugged, but his deep, dark eyes were assessing and thoughtful.

'Far be it from me to tear someone away from her closely held principles,' he murmured.

They headed outside, walking in the balmy summer air in no particular direction.

Except with some surprise Maddie realised that her

legs were somehow moving towards the honeycomb of streets where her grandfather's house was. It was on the outskirts of the city centre and, whilst the location was to die for, the house was not nearly as grand as some of the others and was in a state of disrepair.

The old man, so she had been told by her solicitor, had gradually downsized over the years, more and more as his healthy income had been whittled away to next to nothing, lost in gambling dens and crates of whiskey.

Maddie had wondered whether the absence of his only child had perhaps fuelled that spiral of despair, which had made her even more motivated to accept the challenge that had been bequeathed to her.

She stole a sneaky glance at the towering, over-the-top, sex-on-legs guy next to her and suddenly felt ashamed that she had snapped at him for trying to be a gentleman when in all likelihood he couldn't afford it any more than she could.

'Sorry,' she apologised sheepishly. 'You hit a sore spot there.'

Leo paused and looked down at her, holding her eyes with his, his expression speculative.

Her body trembled as she gazed back up at him, her eyes undoubtedly betraying her want.

'I'll be on my way,' Leo murmured, breaking eye contact to stare up the road which was still as busy now as it had been hours previously. New York was not the only city, it would seem, that never slept.

'Leo…' Maddie breathed.

She wanted him. She didn't know whether it was because she was lonely or because the unexpected stirring of attraction had reminded her that she was still young after all. Maybe he had unlocked some realisation that she couldn't remain a prisoner of her past for the rest of her life.

Or maybe he was just so damned sexy that she simply couldn't resist the pull of raw, primal lust.

Two ships passing in the night, she thought…

'Do you want me to kiss you?' Leo asked on a husky murmur, still not touching her.

'No!' Thank goodness they had managed to find themselves in a quiet corner of the otherwise busy street.

'Then you need to stop looking at me like that.'

'Like what?'

'Like you want to eat me up…like you'd like *me* to eat *you* up.'

'Leo…'

'We're both adults,' Leo delivered on a rough undertone, 'so I'll be honest. You're spectacular-looking and I want you more than I can remember wanting any woman for a long time. I want to touch you. I want to taste you…*everywhere.* But I don't do long-term and in this instance we're talking a one-night stand. A one-night stand to remember, but still a one-night stand. If you don't like that, then walk away, Maddie.'

'I always promised myself that I would never have a one-night stand,' Maddie said, by rote, but her body was certainly not walking away. Indeed, it was staying very firmly put.

Leo shrugged, holding her gaze.

Confusion tore through Maddie, because she wasn't lying. She'd never been a one-night stand kind of girl. From a young age her looks had attracted attention, and she had learned very fast that attention from the opposite sex more often than not bypassed the important stuff—like getting to know her, giving her credit for having a brain and seeing beyond the fact that she was, in Leo's words, 'spectacular-looking'. Adam had only served to cement those lessons in her head.

But…

But, but, but…

'Would you like to come in for a cup of coffee?' she hazarded.

Leo's eyebrows shot up. He refused to let her hide behind the cup of coffee scenario. 'You want me. And I want you. I'll accept the offer of coffee, but I'm not interested in a push-pull game of one step forward followed by two back.'

'Nor am I.' She tiptoed forward, filled with a sense of heady daring, and brushed his perfect mouth with hers.

CHAPTER THREE

AFTER A BRISK walk away from the city centre, they found themselves in a tree-lined avenue filled with mansions.

'I don't live in one of these.'

Maddie didn't look at him as she said this but her cheeks were flaming red. She wasn't lying, but she was uncomfortably conscious of the fact that she had played fast and loose with the truth.

She consoled herself with the obvious justification that launching into a garbled, long-winded explanation about inheritances and distant relatives was not relevant, given they were not going to be in one another's lives for longer than this one night.

Which brought her full circle, questioning what she was doing. A one-night stand? Her proud, stubborn, fiercely independent mother would have had a heart attack on the spot, because she had drummed it into her only child that you had to choose carefully when it came to giving your body to someone else.

'You'll make mistakes,' Lizzie Gallo had told her daughter, 'but it's still important to go into every relationship thinking it could be the one.'

Reflecting now on that advice, Maddie had to concede that her mother might not have ended up where she had, if she'd a one-night stand with Maddie's father rather than running away with him, only to be abandoned the second he realised that the fortune he'd banked on Lizzie's father providing wasn't going to be coming his way.

Disinheritance in the name of love hadn't been his thing. He'd stuck around just long enough to determine that there was going to be no reconciliation between daughter and rich daddy, and then he'd scarpered.

'But I gave it my all,' her mother had said, in one of her rare moments of honesty—because Lizzie Gallo had never been someone to moan and look backwards. 'And, for me, that was the main thing. You climb into bed with someone for a few hours and, believe me, you won't feel great when you climb out of it so that you can do the walk of shame back home.'

Well, that, Maddie reflected, sneaking a sidelong glance at the virtual stranger who had somehow managed to ensnare her into jettisoning all her principles, had not exactly served her well when it came to Adam.

She'd thrown herself into her relationship with Adam and given it everything. She'd been so in love with the idea of being in love that she'd missed all the warning signs of a relationship that had been made anywhere but in heaven.

This time… *This time she knew what she was getting into.* No girlish fantasies and romantic daydreams about Prince Charming only for Prince Charming to turn out to be Mr Toad. She was with a guy who wasn't interested in laying down roots and who'd made it perfectly clear what he wanted.

She felt the bloom of longing between her legs and swallowed down a rush of powerful excitement.

The houses they were passing now were getting smaller and finally, at the end of the elegant road, she swung up the only drive that was unkempt.

'Not what I expected.' Leo glanced at the edifice of what must once upon a time been a rather charming cottage but now looked like something from the Land that Time Forgot.

'What did you expect?'

Maddie unlocked the front door and pushed it open into a hallway that was worn, but still carried the hallmarks of the house it had once been. A flagstone floor, an old-fashioned wooden umbrella stand, a sturdy banister leading upstairs, and worn paintwork with great big discoloured patches from where she had removed dark, lugubrious paintings.

'Something a little less…imposing…'

'Does that bother you?'

'Why should it?'

She'd turned to look at him and Leo could not resist the urge to touch, to feel the smoothness of her cheeks. He ran an exploratory finger over her striking cheekbones and then outlined the contours of her full mouth. When she shivered, he smiled with undisguised hunger.

'I don't know how you do what you do to me,' he murmured, trailing his finger down towards her tee shirt and stopping just where the shadow of her cleavage began, 'but all I want to do right now is rip those clothes off you and take you right here, right now…'

Maddie's breath caught in her throat and she unconsciously arched her body up, so that her small, high breasts pushed towards him in a bold invitation for him to touch.

It was clear she wanted him—so badly that it was a physical ache—and her whole body shuddered as he slipped his hand underneath her tee shirt and then cupped her breast briefly, before tugging the lacy bra to one side so that he could feel the softness of her skin and the tightness of her nipple.

Positioning himself in front of her, Leo reached under the shirt with both hands, pushing up her bra completely to free her breasts, all the while keeping his eyes firmly pinned to her face, because he was absolutely loving the mesmerised hot burn of desire in her bright green eyes.

He stroked her nipples with the pads of his thumbs and her lips parted on a sigh of pleasure.

'Liking it?'

'Don't stop.'

If *he* couldn't understand the primal urgency of his reaction to her, then the same must be said for her. Leo didn't need any more encouragement. He removed her tee shirt in one easy movement and for a few seconds just looked at her perfect breasts, no more than a handful, tipped with rosy buds. His erection was hard and heavy and painful, and he had to breathe in deep to control the fierce sweep of lust.

Her head was flung back, her eyes closed as he slowly backed her towards the staircase, and then she was standing, holding on to the banister, her body beautifully positioned for him to attend to her naked breasts.

Which he did.

He suckled one stiffened nipple, licking and teasing it with his tongue, while he readied the other for his ministrations with his fingers. Her soft moans were doing all sorts of wonderful things to his body and right now he couldn't get enough of her. It was remarkable.

Leaving one throbbing nipple behind, he gave a repeat performance on the other, drawing it deep into his mouth while his tongue continued to torment her.

Maddie reached down to undo the button of his jeans but Leo stopped her.

He would have liked to kid himself that this was to do with his mastering the situation and taking his time, but he had to admit wryly to himself that it was more to do with breaking things off briefly so that he could gather his crazily scattered self-control. Any more touching and he would have to fight not to explode without warning.

'What about the coffee?' he reminded her shakily, and Maddie blinked, roused from her slumberous enjoyment and clearly desperate for him to carry on touching her.

'Coffee?' she parroted weakly, which actually made Leo burst out laughing.

He kissed her on the mouth—a teasing, gentle kiss that made her squirm because it was so tender.

'You can't promise a man coffee and then renege on the offer...'

'Of course not.'

Maddie grinned and slung her arms around his neck to pull him towards her, before shuffling her heated body back into her bra and tee shirt while he watched with avid, devouring hunger. Then she reached out to pepper his sexy mouth with little, darting kisses before slipping her tongue in.

'You're a witch,' he muttered against her mouth.

In the grip of a situation he could never have predicted, Leo followed her towards the back of the house and into a kitchen which, as with the rest of what he'd seen, was in dire need of attention.

'Tell me what you're doing in a house like this,' Leo said, his eyes returning to her slender frame, her back towards him as she made them both mugs of coffee.

Maddie stilled, but only for a fraction of a second, and then she said lightly, 'I can thank a relative for the use of this house. It's not much, but it's brilliant just having a roof over my head. Even a roof that springs leaks when it rains. You should see the corridor upstairs. I've learned just where to position the buckets and pans.' She spun round to hand him his mug. 'You never told me whether it bothers you?'

'I believe I said, why should it?'

'Well,' she said, 'you might get it into your head that I'm a snob because I happen to be staying in a house like this. You might think that we're from different worlds and that wouldn't be the case.'

'Whether it's the case or not,' Leo countered smoothly, 'it doesn't really matter, does it? We're here to enjoy ourselves, not analyse one another's beliefs.'

He let her lead the way into a sitting room, where she opted for switching on one of the lamps on the table rather than the overhead light.

The sofas were deep and squashy, but there were an abnormal amount of small tables and a feeling of a place stuck in time. Leo had no idea where this helpful relative was, but he sincerely hoped he was on an urgent spending spree to replace the furnishings.

He placed his cup on one of the many tables and sat next to her on one of the sofas. Sprawled against one end, he crooked his finger and she wriggled up towards him. He swivelled her so that she was lying against him, her back pressed against his body, nicely pushing down on his hard, thick erection.

He took her coffee from her and settled them both into a more comfortable position.

If this house belonged to him, he decided on the spot, he would put a floor-to-ceiling mirror on the opposite wall for an occasion such as this, when he would have enjoyed nothing better than seeing their reflection, watching the little changes on her beautiful face as he touched her.

He removed the tee shirt once more, wondering why she had bothered to put it back on in the first place when it was always just going to come off again, and cupped her breasts in his hands, playing with them and working her up bit by bit.

Looking down at her, with the soft, flowery scent of her hair filling his nostrils, Leo could see the faint blush of her skin. She was still golden, but paler where her clothes had protected her from the sun, and against the paleness of her breasts her nipples were deep rosy discs. He badly wanted to suckle on them again but he would wait.

At least, he reflected wryly, he wasn't on the verge of coming prematurely. A temporary reprieve from the unthinkable.

She was wearing button-fly jeans and he began undoing the buttons one at a time until he could glimpse her white knickers.

'Take your jeans off,' he murmured. 'I'd do it myself, but my hands are otherwise occupied at the moment.'

He moved them back to her breasts as she wriggled

out of the jeans, leaving her underwear on. The jeans fell to the floor and then she squirmed a little, like a cat preparing to settle on a feather cushion. She reached up and began to turn around, but he stilled her with his hands, silently instructing her to stay as she was.

'I'm hanging on to my self-control by a thread,' he confided. 'Turn around and I won't be able to predict what might happen. Your eyes do something to me...'

Maddie laughed. And as his hand moved from breast to ribcage she parted her legs and whimpered with pleasure.

'I wish I could see your face,' Leo said huskily, and she laughed again.

'I'm glad you can't. I'd be embarrassed.'

Leo grunted. He was accustomed to flamboyant women who weren't easily embarrassed—and certainly not by antics between the sheets. He found her diffidence a turn-on.

Gently he slipped his hand underneath her white panties, felt the brush of downy hair against his fingers, and as he slid one long brown finger into her wetness he couldn't prevent a groan of pure sensual enjoyment.

He found the throbbing bud and she moaned as he began playing with it. She parted her legs further and he cupped her briefly before carrying on with what he'd been doing.

Maddie feverishly wriggled out of her underwear. Sensation was tearing into her and she found that she could scarcely breathe. When she looked down to see the motion of his hand as he played with her she wanted to pass out from the sheer erotic pleasure of it.

Letting go of the last of her inhibitions, she gave herself over to what he was doing to her body. The rhythmic stroke of his finger against her core was taking her higher and higher, and her breathing was staccato as she moved against his hand, bucking and arching, and then, as a low groan was wrenched out of her, she toppled over the edge and spasmed against his fingers in an orgasm that went on and on and on, an unstoppable spiral of pleasure.

Spent, Maddie lay against him, her eyes closed. And then, as she floated back to earth, she turned around and straddled him.

Strangely, she wanted him even more now, but she would have to give her body time to recover. She linked her fingers behind his neck and smiled.

'That was…wonderful…' she confessed.

Leo placed his hands on her waist. He could very nearly circle it with his hands, she was so slender.

'For me too.'

'I'm sorry. It was selfish of me to come, but I couldn't hold off.'

'I didn't want you to,' he said roughly. 'You'll come again, but next time I'll be deep inside you, and when you do I'll see your face and watch when the moment happens.'

Maddie blushed, because she had never indulged in this sort of sexual banter, and the way he was holding her gaze was such a turn-on that she could almost come again without him having to touch her.

She buried her face against the side of his neck and felt a pang, something so sharp and painful that she almost drew back—a pang of *missing*.

She swept that silly feeling aside and this time *she* was the one to touch and arouse. She stripped him of his clothing, looked in wonder at his impressive size. When she ordered him to lie back on the sofa, he laughed.

'I guess we should migrate upstairs to a bed,' she said at one point, in between licking him, teasing him with her mouth and kissing him.

'Why? This sofa does very nicely indeed...'

Was that because a sofa somehow carried on the one-night stand theme? Maddie wondered.

She lost herself in the wonder of his glorious body. He was lean and strong, and the dark hair on his chest felt like a declaration of masculinity. He was all man. Alpha male to the very core of him. And she couldn't get enough of his body, of *him*.

This time things moved at a pace that allowed them to explore one another as if they had all the time in the world.

Where his fingers had been, his mouth explored. He tasted between her thighs until she was practically crying for him to take her all the way. She tasted him as well, and his hands curled into her long hair, directing her so that she knew what felt good for him—although she quickly discovered that she seemed to have a second sense for pleasing him.

Or maybe it was simply the fact that the novelty of this situation had made him so aroused that whatever she did and wherever she touched it would have the same dramatic effect.

Leo wanted to hang on. Hell, it shouldn't be a problem. He was a master when it came to self-control in the bedroom—a guy who knew how to orchestrate sex and time it to perfection. Not so now.

He couldn't hang on. He couldn't find his self-control or *any* kind of control for that matter. He couldn't think. He just had to have her before he splintered into a million pieces.

Whatever world he had entered, it was in a different league from anything he had ever experienced in his life before. Savage want poured through his body in waves that carried the ferocity of a sledgehammer, knocking him for six and wiping out his formidable composure.

The disconnect between his head and his body had never been greater, but all that was forgotten when he thrust into her and felt her body arch up to meet his, moulding and fitting against him as smoothly as a hand fitted into a glove personally made for it.

Leo felt as though she had been fashioned for him, her body so perfectly tuned to his that the straightforward business of making love was elevated into an experience beyond description.

His climax was the most powerful he had ever had, and he only surfaced when it was over and his body was well and truly spent. Then he turned her to face him so that their naked bodies were pressed together.

'Maddie...' The self-control that had been left at the front door now made its presence known. 'We didn't... *hell*...' He groaned aloud and raked his fingers through his hair. 'It's never happened before but I didn't use protection. Are you...this is not be a question I should ever have to ask...but are you on the pill?'

Slumberous green cat's eyes focused on him and she frowned. 'No. No, I'm not.'

How could she have taken a chance like this?

But then, he thought, she'd taken it for the same reason he had. Because lust had been so much more overwhelming than common sense. Their bodies had been on fire and the notion of protection hadn't even registered.

'There's not a lot we can do now…' She sighed and squirmed, the heat of his body already scattering her thoughts and fogging her mind.

Leo was astounded at the speed with which he was prepared to immerse himself in that vague assurance, but he reminded himself that he had friends who'd taken months, and in a couple of cases years, to achieve what he'd always been scrupulous in protecting himself against.

He placed his hand on her waist and shifted. This was a one-night stand. Right about now he should be getting his act together and telling her that it was time for him to go.

'Maddie…'

'I hope you have a good trip back to…to…'

Maddie was quick to silence any little voice that wanted to promote something more than the one-night stand that was on the table.

She feathered a kiss on his mouth. 'To wherever it is you're going next.'

'London.' Leo cleared his throat. 'I'm going straight down to London from here.'

'Well, in that case I hope you have a very good trip back down to London. Say hi to Big Ben for me.' She traced an idle pattern on his hard, naked chest.

'It's possible,' Leo inserted gruffly, without batting an eyelid, 'that I could explore Dublin for a few days, however…'

It could work. He could do a few background checks on the store, fill in the blanks. It wouldn't hurt. And while he was here he could wine and dine this woman who had just made the earth move for him. Wine and dine on a budget, of course, bearing in mind that she thought that he was in the same financial bracket as she was.

The thought held a great deal of appeal for Leo. He wasn't ready to chalk this heady experience down as a one-night stand. He was a man who had always had everything he wanted—and certainly every woman he had ever wanted. Having it all, however, had definite downsides...one of which was a jaded palate. Maddie, from the other side of the world, was like a dose of pure, life-giving oxygen.

Doubtless this sense of exhilaration would wither and die after a couple of nights, because they had absolutely nothing in common and sex, however earth-moving, was just sex after all, but in the meantime...

He pulled her back towards him, wanting her all over again. The more he thought about it, the more appealing was the idea of playing truant for a couple of days, of taking time out from life as he knew it.

'Really? You might stay here for a while?'

Maddie felt as though a cloud she hadn't even realised had been there had suddenly lifted to reveal a bank of unexpected sunshine.

'There's nothing more exciting than exploring a new city.'

'That would be lovely,' Maddie said.

Leo grinned. 'Let's go for a bit more enthusiasm,' he encouraged,

Maddie hesitated. She'd geared herself up for a one-night stand, at the end of which she'd wave goodbye to this stranger who had filled her life with joy for a brief period of time. A two-or three-night stand posed a few more issues, and top of the list was the fact that she hadn't been entirely truthful with him.

'Okay.' She smiled and wriggled against him, and felt the jut of his erection against her belly. 'I'd really like that. But there's something I feel I ought to tell you…'

'Please don't tell me that you're a married woman with a jealous husband hiding in a cupboard somewhere.'

'Of course I'm not!'

'Then what?'

He gently pushed her onto her back and rose up over her, nudging her with the tip of his throbbing erection, swiping it slowly against her core until she was losing track of what she wanted to tell him.

No condoms? No problem. There were myriad ways to pleasure one another without penetration, and in the morning they could stockpile protection.

'I'm not quite who you think I am. I mean, you've got the major details, but there's one little thing… You know the store?'

'The store?' Leo nudged a little further into her moistness, clearly only half registering what she was saying because his body was already taking over and deciding where its priorities lay. *Not* in a heart-to-heart discussion.

'Where we met.'

'Ah, *that* store. What about it?'

'I'm not actually a shop assistant there.'

'No? Shoplifter?'

Maddie laughed. In the short space of time she'd known him she'd found that he had a brilliant sense of humour.

'Owner, as a matter of fact.'

Leo stilled and slowly pulled back so that he was staring down at her, scarcely believing his ears. *'Owner...?'*

Sensing the shift in atmosphere, Maddie laughed nervously. 'It doesn't matter,' she assured him. 'I haven't suddenly turned into a crashing snob.'

'Owner? Please explain. I'm all ears.'

He slung his muscular legs over the side of the sofa and began getting dressed.

Maddie didn't try to stop him—if he wanted to leave then he should leave—but she felt as though a black hole had opened up beneath her feet.

'My grandfather owned the store.'

Maddie was beginning to feel uncomfortable now, and disadvantaged because she was still naked and vulnerable. So she too began to sling on the clothes she had earlier discarded in such excited haste.

From having their bodies pressed so closely together they might have been one, they now stood awkwardly in the dimly lit living room, facing one another like sparring opponents in a ring.

Maddie had no idea why or how this had occurred. But past experience had taught her the wisdom of developing a tough outer shell, and it came into effect now, stiffening her backbone, lending defiance to her glass-green eyes.

'I'm listening,' Leo said softly.

'I never met him. He and my mother fell out before I was born and never reconciled. But when he died a short while back he left the entire store to me, along with this house.' She gestured to encompass the building in which they were standing. 'And a few other bits and pieces. I'm sorry I wasn't upfront with you, but I didn't see the point of launching into my back story.'

'I had no idea…' Leo said slowly.

Tommaso's granddaughter. This changed everything, and already the shutters were falling into place. He didn't believe in age-old enmities, and he certainly didn't believe in taking sides in a feud in which he had played no part, but something stirred in him—a sense of injustice done to his grandfather. Was this what they meant when they said that blood was thicker than water?

That aside, he intended to buy the place—whoever or whatever stood in his way—and the woman standing in front of him now was no longer the lover he wanted to keep in his bed but his adversary in a deal he intended to close.

'I don't see that it changes anything.' Maddie winced at the plea hidden behind her words.

'It changes *everything*,' Leo said softly, heading towards the door.

'Because you've found out I'm not impoverished?' Maddie threw at him, half following, but only because she was so angry and bewildered.

'You'll find out why soon enough…'

Pride held her back and killed the questions rising fast inside her, but when she heard the front door slam she sagged onto the sofa.

She didn't care. He meant nothing to her! She wasn't going to beat herself up about her decision to go to bed with him and she certainly wasn't going to waste time asking herself what he'd meant by that parting shot.

CHAPTER FOUR

MADDIE HAD HUNDREDS of steps to take and a veritable long and winding road to go before she could ever begin to return the store she had inherited to its former glory. But, despite the fact that she had no formal training in business, she discovered she had an innate talent for the work and enjoyed the straightforward process of planning a way forward.

If you could call climbing a mountain straightforward...

Certainly over the next fortnight work occupied her mind to the point where she could almost come close to forgetting about her encounter with Leo.

Almost but not quite.

In the quiet hours she spent in the house, meticulously working out how to pull it apart so that she could put it together again, he invaded her thoughts like a stealthy intruder, finding his way into all the nooks and crannies of her mind.

She had no regrets about what they had done. She had taken a risk and lived in the moment and she had enjoyed every minute of it. But she had to ask herself whether she had somehow inherited her mother's gene for always picking the wrong man. First Adam and then Leo.

With finances for moving forward with the store's

overhaul now in place, thanks to a sympathetic bank manager who was as keen as she to see the store resume its rightful place as the leading light in the city centre, there was just one hurdle left to overcome.

'There's a buyer waiting in the wings,' her lawyer, Anthony, had told her three days previously, 'and he is prepared to be hostile to get the store.'

'Over my dead body.'

The house had been remortgaged, dozens of valuable paintings and artefacts which had been bought when her grandfather had been living in boom times had been sold, and sufficient capital acquired to support the loan from the bank. Maddie had got little sleep while putting it all together, and she wasn't going to have the rug pulled from under her feet at the last minute.

But Anthony had told her that with a good enough offer on the table he would find it hard not to advise a sale. He had then gone into the complexities of the money she was being lent, and interest rates and time frames, and Maddie had zoned out, focusing only on the fight that lay ahead of her.

More than ever, as she fought to get things in order, it seemed to her that she was doing something the grandfather she had never met had intended her to do.

She'd never known what it was like to have any sort of extended family. Her mother had been tight-lipped on the subject of her own family, which had been diminished to just her father by the time she had left for Australia with the man who would eventually turn out to be precisely the fortune-hunter she had been warned against.

Maddie had always secretly felt saddened at the thought of her grandfather perhaps trying to keep in touch. Who knew? Her mother had died relatively young. Perhaps if she hadn't she would have eventually swallowed her pride and returned to England.

Just being in the house where her grandfather had lived had warmed Maddie towards the man she had never known. In her mind he had been a kindly gentleman who had been big-hearted enough to leave all his worldly goods to her.

No one was going to deprive her of her legacy and everything that was wrapped up with it. This slice of her past had completed her—filled in the dots about where she had come from. It wasn't just a business deal for her. It was a reconnection with the past she had never known, and it was giving her a sense of direction and purpose in a life that had always held a lot of unanswered questions.

Which didn't mean that she wasn't feeling sick to her stomach as she and Anthony strode into the imposing glass house on the outskirts of the city centre where a meeting of the buyer's lawyers had been arranged on neutral territory.

'Where are we?' she asked nervously as they entered the building and were faced with grey modernist splendour.

She'd dressed in her most serious outfit, bought especially for the occasion—a sober grey suit, a crisp white shirt and very high black heels that would give her the advantage over any hostile bidder because in her heels she was at least six foot tall. Provided she didn't sit down, she was sure she would appear a sufficiently commanding figure and be able to announce to the assembled crowd that she wasn't someone to be messed with.

She could tell that Anthony, who only just reached her shoulder, approved of the tactic.

She had also pinned her chaotic hair back into a neat chignon that had taken for ever to do and had almost made her late.

'We're within the hallowed walls of one of the most influential companies in the country,' Anthony adjusted his tie a little nervously. 'Mostly building and construction, but recently diversifying into electronics and smart installations in new-builds.'

'Impressive.'

'Our buyer obviously has a lot of connections if he can snap his fingers and arrange for the meeting to be held here. I've done my background research and he's made of money.'

'Well, money isn't everything. Maybe he's trying to intimidate us.'

Maddie told herself that scare tactics weren't going to work, but she was as nervous as a kitten as they were escorted along a cool marble walkway that circled an impressive courtyard, which was visible through banks of glass. When she looked down she could see a few figures dotted around a central fountain, enjoying the sunshine even though it wasn't yet lunchtime.

Then, looking ahead, she saw opaque glass, and as their escort stood aside she entered a long, brightly lit room. *Quite a few men*, was Maddie's first thought. All kitted out in regulation charcoal-grey business suits.

Except one.

One man dominated the space around him and was head and shoulders taller than every other man there. He was not wearing a suit. Black jeans and a black polo shirt, short-sleeved. The epitome of *I don't give a damn what I wear* cool.

Leo.

* * *

Leo had been expecting her, but he still felt a sizzle of something as she walked into the room, towering over the short man next to her, so strikingly pretty that every single male in the room fell silent.

His white teeth snapped together in a surge of something primitive and proprietorial.

He'd had her. She was his.

His woman.

Except, he thought as logic reasserted itself, she wasn't, was she? She was his opponent. And, as such, no time must be wasted on thinking about all her delectable, distracting assets.

His midnight-deep eyes roved broodingly over her. She was wearing the most boring outfit in the world, but even that couldn't stand in the way of his imagination which had already taken flight.

He mentally stripped her. Got rid of the dreadful suit and the prissy top. Unhooked whatever bra she was wearing and pulled down her panties. Why had she tied her hair back? The urge to see it spilling in colourful splendour over her slender shoulders was so powerful that he had to steady himself.

It had been over a fortnight.

He hadn't been braced to walk away from her but walk away he had—because, with him, business always came first. Always had, always would.

There wasn't a woman in the world who could damage that sacred pecking order.

But he knew that he was getting excited just looking at her and thinking about what she'd felt like under him and over him and touching him and inviting him to touch her everywhere.

That sign of weakness enraged him, and he broke the mental connection by stepping forward and walking straight towards her.

It took willpower she had never known she'd possessed to hold her ground and not fall back as the one man she had never expected to see again sauntered towards her.

What on earth was going on?

Maddie knew that whatever impression she was making it wasn't that of a confident businesswoman in charge of the situation. More a gaping goldfish, stranded and gasping for air.

'I don't understand...' She stared at Leo, her breathing rapid and shallow, as though she'd been running a marathon, her nostrils flaring as she inhaled the clean, woody scent of him.

She'd thought about him so much that she could scarcely believe that he was standing in front of her—especially as none of it seemed to make any sense.

Leo didn't say anything for a few seconds, and when he did speak it was to tell the assembled crowd that they could leave.

'I'll deal with this privately,' he said dismissively. 'When the transaction is agreed you can prepare the required paperwork.'

'Maddie... Ms Gallo...' Anthony approached her with an expression of concern—only to meet Leo's cool navy eyes.

'Maddie will be as safe as houses with me,' he said, addressing the much shorter man in a kindly voice that made Maddie's teeth snap together in anger because it was just so...*patronising*.

'Now, wait just a minute...er...'

'Leo. You know my name. You just don't know my surname. Conti.'

'You're…you're…' Her brain was moving at a snail's pace.

Yes, Conti was the name of the man who was planning on pulling the rug from under her feet. Maddie vaguely recalled that much sinking in when Anthony had explained the situation to her. She'd been far too wrapped up in feeling angry that someone could just swan along and try and snatch the store away from her before she'd even had a chance to do something with it.

The men in suits were quietly leaving the room. Maddie was conscious of their departure, but only just—because she was gradually putting two and two together, and by the time the door closed on the lawyers who had come to draw up a deal she had no intention of agreeing to she was fit to explode.

'You *lied* to me!' she burst out, galvanised into action and storming over to the window, then storming back towards him, hands on her hips, eyes spitting fury.

Leo stood his ground and met her tempestuous gaze head-on, without so much as flinching.

'Did I?' he drawled, moving towards the table at the back of the room to pour himself a glass of water, taking his time.

'You let me think that you were…you were… What were you doing in my store in the first place? Oh, don't bother answering that! You'd come along to have a look at what you wanted to get your hands on!'

'I like to see what I'm sinking my money into, yes.'

'I'm leaving!' She spun round, shaking, and began heading towards the door.

She didn't get there, because two strides in she was stopped by his hand on her arm.

Her whole body reacted as though a shot of high-voltage electricity had been injected straight into her bloodstream. The heat from his hand would have been enough to stop her dead in her tracks even if no pressure had been applied.

Her body remembered his and that terrified her.

'How could you have lied to me!'

Leo met her vivid eyes. 'Stop playing the crucified martyr, Maddie. Have you conveniently forgotten that you weren't exactly forthcoming about who *you* were when we were climbing into the sack together?'

'That was different!'

'How? Enlighten me?'

'I thought you might have been scared off because I happened to own the store! *Ha!*'

'Is that right? And if I'd told you who I was…would we have ended up in bed?'

'I'm getting the picture, Leo. You're rich and powerful and you were scared that a poor little salesgirl might have decided you were a promising candidate to get involved with…'

'Is that so far-fetched?'

Maddie stared stubbornly at him, too angry to give an inch on this, even though she could see that he might, conceivably, have a point.

Not that it mattered! What mattered was that he was not going to get his rich, powerful paws on the store her grandfather had left her.

'Well?' Leo pressed, his tone making it clear he felt she was equally guilty of deception to suit her own purposes.

'If you knew me *at all,*' Maddie snapped, 'then you

would know that the fact you're rich doesn't work in your favour. If you'd told me from the start who you were and what you were worth I would have run a mile! I've had enough experience of rich creeps to last me a lifetime!'

Leo's eyes narrowed.

He'd loosened his grip on her arm but he was still holding her, and the look in his eyes was saying he wanted to do so much more than just hold her.

Their eyes locked and she felt a shift in the atmosphere from blazing anger to the slow sizzle of sexual awareness.

She found that she was holding her breath.

'Don't,' Maddie whispered.

'Don't what?'

'Look at me like that.'

'You mean the way you're looking at me? As though the only thing on your mind now is the thought of my mouth on yours?'

She wrenched herself free from his grasp and took a few shaky steps back.

'Don't kid yourself!'

She wrapped her arms around her body to stop herself from shaking like a leaf. He was so big, so powerful, and she was so drawn to him that she had to make a conscious effort not to stumble back into his hypnotic radius like a zombie under the spell of a master magician.

'Like I said, I don't go for guys like you!'

Guys like him?

Leo was enraged to be categorised and written off. He was even more enraged that his body was reacting to her like a sex-starved, randy adolescent when his brain was telling him to drop any pointless back-and-forth conversation and get down to business.

'That's not what you were saying a fortnight ago, when you fell into my arms like a starving person suddenly presented with a five-course spread.'

The erection pushing against the zipper of his jeans was as hard as steel and he abruptly turned away, giving himself time to get his runaway libido under control.

'I made a mistake with a rich man,' Maddie flung at him in a trembling voice. 'I got involved with someone I thought had a conscience and a moral compass and I discovered that, actually, rich people don't operate like that. Rich people are above the law, and they don't give a damn who they step on because they know they're never going to have to pay the price for what they do!'

Leo stared at her through narrowed eyes. 'You're judging me by someone you happen to have been involved with who...*what*? Did a runner? Hit on your best friend?'

'If only,' Maddie said bitterly. 'Oh, Adam White was a lot more destructive than *that*!'

She seemed to catch herself and fell silent, breathing evenly as if to stifle the emotions which had definitely got the better of her.

'It doesn't matter,' she told him coolly. 'What matters is that I'm not going to be selling you the store and I don't care how much money you throw down on the table.'

'Sit.'

'I'm perfectly fine standing.'

'Let's put our brief liaison behind us, Maddie. What's at stake here has nothing to do with the fact that we slept together. We're both adults. It happened. Neither of us knew the full story when we climbed into bed. Or should I say when we occupied the sofa in your sitting room.'

The evocative image his words conjured did nothing

to lessen the surge of his unwanted attraction. Leo carried on without skipping a beat, but he had to divert his eyes from her face. Even the fact that she was glaring at him couldn't diminish her pulling power.

'There's no point playing the blame game. Okay, so you might have run a mile if you'd known how rich I was.' He shrugged indifferently. 'And maybe I didn't advertise my wealth because I've had experience of what it's like to be targeted by women who only have one thing on their mind.'

'Oh, please,' Maddie muttered sarcastically.

Leo raised his eyebrows to look at her. 'You think I'm lying?'

'Don't pretend that you don't know how attractive you are—with or without your stupid oversized bank balance!'

Leo shot her a slow, curling smile and the atmosphere was suddenly charged. She flicked her tongue over her upper lip and the gesture was so *sexy* that Leo found himself stepping towards her.

She didn't pull back. She couldn't, because her legs had turned to lead. She almost whimpered when he was only inches away from her, but fortunately pride kicked in and instead she drew a steadying breath and tried to clear her mind from the fog enveloping it.

'Tough, isn't it?' Leo drawled huskily, and the low, velvety timbre of his voice sent shivers racing up and down her spine.

'I don't know what you're talking about.'

But she was mesmerised by his eyes and the sheer beauty of his face. He had the most amazing lashes, she thought distractedly—so long, so thick. It was just another detail to take in and store.

She balled her hands into defensive fists and made a concerted effort to drag her wayward mind back from the brink—which was a very, *very* dangerous place for it to stray.

'Oh, you know exactly what I'm talking about, Maddie. The thing our bodies are doing right now. Don't try and pretend that you don't want me to touch you right here, right now, and damn the consequences.' Then he drew back abruptly and said, his voice brisk, 'But that's not going to do. Business before pleasure, I'm afraid.'

He grinned and her humiliation was complete.

How could she have allowed herself to forget that this was her enemy? Another rich man who had lied to her? A man who wanted to take what was hers and was willing to do so by whatever means he deemed fit? A bully, in other words.

She blinked and glared and wanted nothing more badly than to wipe the grin from his face—not least because it just ratcheted up his outrageous sex appeal.

'I suppose,' Leo drawled, stepping away and sauntering towards the window, where he proceeded to glance out before returning his full attention to her face, 'your lawyer, or your accountant, or whoever that little man was who came in with you, has explained the deal that's been put on the table?'

'I didn't pay much attention to that because I'm not interested in selling.'

'Big mistake. You should have. Sentiment is all well and good, but money is what does the talking—and I'm prepared to put however much money down on the table I have to if it gets me what I want. And believe me when I tell you that my supply of cash is bottomless.'

He'd gone into that store fully prepared to pay the

least amount of money for the place he could, but he was fast revising his original plan because she was stubborn and—for reasons that frankly confounded him—she wasn't going to roll over and play dead because he wanted her to.

He felt a sense of grudging admiration, because people, as a rule, were prone to caving in to him in the face of any show of determination, such was the range of his power and influence and the force of his personality.

She, on the other hand, looked as close to caving in as his art teacher had looked when, at the age of ten, Leo had asked to be let off detention because the dog had eaten his project.

'Maddie, you could have your dream life with the money I'm prepared to offer. Frankly, as it stands, I would be handing over far more than the place is worth. Because in case you haven't noticed it's falling apart at the seams and it's lost its customer base. One more poor season and the whole house of cards will come tumbling down.'

'I've sorted out the finances and I have a business plan to get it back up and running.'

'Impressive. I had no idea you had experience in bringing ailing companies back from the brink.'

'This is more than just a game for me, Leo. I never met my grandfather and yet he placed his faith in me to transform the store.'

'The store that *he* ran into the ground because of his fondness for the bottle and the nearest gambling den.'

Maddie stiffened. If he thought that he was going to get to her by insulting her grandfather then he was mistaken. Yes, Tommaso Gallo had drunk too much and gambled away his fortune, but she was convinced that

that was because he had lost his only daughter. That was what misery could do to a person.

'Why are you so keen to have it, Leo?' She shot him a look of helpless frustration. 'Why can't you just buy something else? Somewhere else? I mean, it's a *store*. If you're sarcastic about *my* lack of business experience, then how much experience in retail do *you* have?'

She realised that she actually had no idea what he did for a living or where his money came from.

Leo was staring at her thoughtfully. Her sentiments seemed to be skewed. Did she somehow see herself as the beneficiary of a kindly old Father Christmas figure? She'd never met the old man, and clearly had no idea of the sort of person he was.

Should he break the glad tidings that Tommaso Gallo and Father Christmas had about as much in common as a rattlesnake and a mouse?

He decided that revelations could wait until another day. He pushed himself away from the window and flexed his muscles as he prowled through the vast conference room, finally sinking into one of the leather chairs and swivelling it so that it was facing her.

'I wouldn't keep it as the same type of traditional retail store.'

Strangely, despite her high heels and the fact that, standing up, she was towering over him, he had shed nothing of his dominance. If anything, she felt awkward standing, so she in turn sat at the very end of the long, walnut table.

At least she now felt more businesslike. 'What would you do to it?'

'I want a foothold in Dublin,' Leo said flatly. 'This store is exactly where I want to be and it's exactly the right size. I have a portfolio of companies and it would continue being a store, but exclusively dealing with my targeted software, adapted high-tech computers and specialised training stations.'

'An electronics shop?'

Leo frowned. 'The retail market is saturated, Maddie. Too many people are buying too many products online. You'll never find a better offer than the one I'm prepared to give you. Take it and don't fight me.'

'Surely you can source another big store to gobble up!'

'You have your personal reasons for wanting to hang on to your white elephant. I have my own personal reasons for wanting to take it from you.'

'What are you talking about?'

'You don't know much about old Tommaso, do you?'

'You *knew* my grandfather?' Confused, Maddie stared at him in consternation. 'How *old* are you?'

Leo smiled drily. 'I'm not an eighty-year-old man rescued from looking his age thanks to plastic surgery.'

'I didn't think you were.'

'And no, to answer your first question, I never met the old man.'

'Then how do you…? I don't understand.'

'My grandfather and Tommaso were friends back in the day. Did your mother never talk about what went on between them?'

'No. No, she didn't.'

'Not a word?'

'I think that part of her life was something she walked away from, and when she walked away she made sure never to look back. I knew she'd fallen out with my grandfather over her choice of partner, and had exiled herself on the other side of the world, but beyond that I really don't know anything about either of my grandparents. *Or* their friends.'

'Well, he and my grandfather were, once upon a time, very good friends. Indeed, they landed in Ireland searching for the same thing,—their fortunes.'

'What was your father called?'

'Benito. Benito and Tommaso. Two friends as tight as thieves until a simple bet tore their friendship apart.'

'A *bet*?' Maddie shook her head. She had no idea where this was heading, but her gut instinct was telling her that wherever it was it wasn't going to be her idea of a dream destination.

'One bet over a certain small shop. The toss of a coin. My grandfather won the bet.'

'But…'

'I know,' Leo purred with an undercurrent of coolness. 'You're asking yourself how it is that Tommaso ended up with the iconic store in Dublin when he lost the bet. I'll tell you how. Your grandfather betrayed Benito. While he was planning what to do with the shop Tommaso hit the bank, secured a loan and made the deal in record time—and then he put his hands up in mock surrender so that he could take his punishment safe in the knowledge that he'd got what he wanted. So you see—you have *your* reasons for hanging on and I have *my* reasons for making sure to loosen your grip. My grandfather has wanted that store for decades. It's just about the only thing he has left to want. He's never stopped trying to get it, and I intend to make sure he gets it before he dies.'

Leo thought that technically, the store wasn't *quite* the only thing his grandfather had left to want. The pitter-patter of tiny great-grandchildren's feet was also high on the old man's wish list—but that was something that wasn't going to happen.

Not given to introspection, and certainly not given to rehashing a past he wanted to forget, Leo was suddenly reminded of the one and only catastrophe that had provided him with the most valuable learning curve he had ever experienced.

Forget about deals and money and what one power broker might be saying to another power broker in order to undermine him. In the great scheme of things, how did *that* figure? No, *his* learning curve had been at the hands of a woman.

He'd been twenty-three, cocksure and confident that he knew all there was to know about women. She'd been ten years older, and what she knew hadn't yet registered on his radar. She'd been sexy, offhand, and she'd made him work. She'd made him work all the way up the aisle into a marriage that had ended before the ink on the certificate had had time to dry.

The alluring, enigmatic sexy woman he'd married had turned out to be a wily fortune-hunter who'd known just what tricks to play on a young rich kid with too much self-confidence and too little cynicism.

After two years she'd relinquished her band of gold in exchange for financial security for the rest of her life.

Leo still kept a picture of her in his wallet—because everybody needed a reminder of their youthful folly.

Afterwards, he'd wondered whether he hadn't been subconsciously ripe for the picking because his grandmother, desperately ill at the time, had been so keen for him to settle down. He'd gone into something and it hadn't been with his eyes wide open.

Thankfully his grandmother had died before she

could witness the true horror of Leo's divorce proceedings and all mention of those pitter-pattering little feet had been dropped, but Leo knew that it was something his grandfather still secretly longed for. He still nurtured a burning desire to see his one and only grandson settled with some plump homely wife who would be there to keep the home fires burning.

Not going to happen.

But number two on the list *could* happen.

'I don't believe you.' Maddie glared at him defiantly. 'The world doesn't need another electronics store. My grandfather's place adds to the history of this city and I'm never—repeat, *never*—going to sell it to you or to anyone else. And I don't care *how* much money you throw at me!'

She was furious on so many levels that she could scarcely breathe. Furious that he had tried to destroy the image she had in her head of her grandfather. But of course he would try any low trick in the book to get what he wanted! Furious that he was so unfazed by every single thing she'd said to him. And furious that he still had that stupid, *stupid* effect on her even though she absolutely *hated* him!

'Is that the sound of a gauntlet being thrown down?' Leo drawled, enjoying the hectic colour in her cheeks and wanting more than anything else to kiss her into submission in just the sort of crazy, macho way he really should have no time for.

'Yes, it is!'

'Fine.' Leo shrugged and began sauntering towards the door. 'In that case…game on.'

CHAPTER FIVE

LEO LOOKED AT the report sitting in front of him. It was slight, but significant. Three pages at most. In the week since he'd seen Maddie he'd had time to reflect on what approach he wanted to take with regard to the store.

'I won't rest until I have it.'

That was what his grandfather had declared only days before, when Leo had presented him with the obstacle in his way in the form of one very beautiful, very stubborn and ridiculously fiery girl from the other side of the world.

'It's a matter of pride. I was fair to Tommaso when he started haemorrhaging money because of the gambling and the drinking. I knew about his wife, knew how unexpected her death was and how hard it'd hit him, and I felt sorry for what the man was going through. We'd been friends, after all. But time and bitterness and pain had turned him into a vengeful old man. He would rather have seen the store fall into rack and ruin than sell it to me—even though I offered way above market price for it—just like he sliced his daughter out of his life rather than forgive and move on. Forget what the granddaughter says about hanging on to it because it's part of the city's heritage. Rubbish! Tommaso couldn't have given a damn about heritage! He refused to sell through sheer spite. He never forgave me because I refused to accept what he had done—refused to accept that he had betrayed me and I'd called him a dishonourable cheat!'

Leo was quietly pleased that his grandfather had still insisted on the purchase. Had he not insisted it was possible that he, Leo, would have shrugged and walked away because he couldn't be bothered with the fight. He would have simply bided his time, waited a couple of years until the place was collapsing—because how successful was it going to be, really, when Maddie hadn't the first idea about running a business—and moved in for the kill.

But she'd thrown down a gauntlet. That was something Leo had never been able to resist.

And more than that… The thought of Maddie being the instigator of the challenge frankly thrilled him.

He hadn't been able to dislodge the woman from his head, where she seemed to have taken up semi-permanent residence. Walking away from her might just have been more frustrating than walking away from the purchase.

And now, in front of him, he had just what he needed to get what he wanted. The trump card, in a manner of speaking. The ace of spades.

To play it or not to play it…?

He would see how their meeting went.

This time he had invited her to his own offices in London. No accountants would be present…no high-powered lawyers.

'We need to talk,' he had drawled when he had called

her two evenings previously. 'I have some information you might find of interest…'

He had heard the hesitation in her voice when she had demanded to know what he could possibly have of interest when she had already said all there was to say on the matter.

He'd had his doubts that she would show up, in which case he would be prepared to simply go and get her, but to his surprise she had texted him only a few hours ago to confirm the meeting and added,

I have something to tell you as well.

When he had tried calling her she had failed to pick up.

And now here he was, and he hadn't been so invigorated in as long as he could remember.

When his PA buzzed to tell him that his visitor had arrived and was waiting in the foyer downstairs, he relaxed back into his chair and smiled to himself, savouring the tingle of anticipation.

'Show her up in fifteen minutes.'

After all, a little bit of mind-games never went amiss…

Downstairs, Maddie was trying hard to squash the painful sensation of nausea rippling through her in little waves. It was like seasickness except far, far worse.

What did Leo want to see her about? What did he have to say that he thought might be of interest? Would he offer more money?

As things stood, Anthony was already getting cold feet about her plan to keep the store, and she'd had to endure a long, meaningful chat about the importance of at least *considering* the very generous offer Leo had made. There was only so far the very loyal investors would agree to it, he had said. In the end they were only human, and if enough money was thrown at them, they would start leaving the sinking ship in droves.

Maddie knew that she would have to be as cool as a cucumber and stand her ground. Except…

She felt another wave of nausea and knew it had nothing to do with the financial discussions ahead of her. Feeling faint now, she closed her eyes briefly and tried not to relive the shock of finding out that she was pregnant.

How *could* she have been so reckless? She'd thought the chances were slim when they'd made love, but the possibility of pregnancy had begun nibbling away at the edges of her mind. Beneath all the angst over the store, and her even greater angst at her chaotic feelings towards Leo, there had been a dragging fear that that one slip-up might have had repercussions.

Even so, she'd been convinced when she'd done a test that she couldn't be *that* unlucky. Wasn't there a limit to how much bad luck one person could have in a life-time? Surely she'd used up her allowance?

Seemingly not.

Little did he know, but one more euro on the table and she would have to relinquish her dream of resur-recting the store and carrying on the legacy her grand-father had left her.

How could she gamble on making a success of some-thing she had never done before when, with a baby in-side her, taking a gamble was the one thing she couldn't afford to do now?

But Maddie wasn't going to think of worst-case scenarios. Not yet.

She sat.

She waited.

And she grew more and more nervous with each passing second.

If he'd wanted to intimidate her he'd chosen his venue well, because this was luxury on a scale that was practically unimaginable. Looking around her, she could tell that even the tiniest of details, like the potted plant on the smoked glass table in front of her, was pricey.

The *people* looked pricey! All young and beautiful in sharp suits, scuttling to and from the bank of elevators on a mission to make more and more money.

She jumped when someone suddenly stood in front of her and told her to follow.

She'd been sitting around for over a quarter of an hour, but instead of the delay giving time for her nerves to settle it had had the opposite effect.

'Mr Conti apologises for the delay in seeing you,' said the forty-something woman with the severe hair cut but kindly face as she preceded Maddie to one of the elevators.

Maddie very much doubted that, but she remained silent, too overawed by her surroundings and too wrapped up with what she was going to say to Leo to say anything at all.

But even in her distraught, anxious daze she couldn't help but notice the details of his vast offices—the smell and feel of money beyond most people's wildest imaginations.

The lift was a deep walnut with smoked glass, and

when it stopped they were disgorged into a huge glass space where workstations were separated by glass partitions and exotic plants. It was predominantly white, and there were a lot of sleek, wafer-thin computers on desks where everyone was hard at work. In fact, no one even glanced across as they walked away from what almost looked like a greenhouse with industrious worker bees towards a more intimate area.

The offices of the CEO were private, and concealed behind walnut and chrome doors. Nerves building to a peak, Maddie nearly turned tail and ran when they finally paused in front of them, closed at the very end of the plush, wide corridor.

'Don't be nervous.' The PA turned to her with a smile and a wink. 'Deep down, he's a lamb.' She paused. 'Well, perhaps *lamb* isn't quite the word I'm looking for, but he's scrupulously fair.'

'I'm not nervous,' Maddie lied, her teeth all but chattering.

Her stomach was in knots as she was propelled through a vast outer office—grey, white and glass—through an interconnecting door and then she was there. Standing in front of him while behind her the door quietly clicked shut.

Maddie stared. She couldn't help herself. The real-life Leo Conti was so much more powerful, so much more breathtaking than the two-dimensional one who had dominated her thoughts for the past couple of weeks since she had seen him.

Her mouth went dry and every single coherent thought vanished from her head, zapped into the ether by the devastating effect he had on her.

'Why don't you have a seat?' Leo said politely.

He wondered whether she was looking at him like that on purpose. Was she trying to turn him on?

Just like that his thoughts veered off at a tantalising tangent.

She wanted the store and, as she'd said, that *want* was wrapped up in all sorts of motivations that had nothing to do with money.

What if she'd decided that stubborn refusal and a fight was the wrong approach to get what she wanted? What if she'd decided that a more powerful weapon was sex?

The drab outfit, a replica of the one she had worn at the last meeting she had attended, certainly didn't advertise a woman prepared to bare her all as a means to an end, but strangely it was even more provocative than if she'd worn a mini-skirt and stilettoes.

Leo toyed with that pleasurable notion in the space of the few seconds it took for her to sink into a chair which was strategically slightly lower than the one in which he was sitting.

He imagined her coming on to him, offering herself to him. He pictured that interconnecting door being locked and his PA dispatched while he stripped her, very, very slowly, and took her even more slowly on his desk…on the sofa in his outer chamber…on the floor…

Sudden craving surged through him and he had to breathe evenly and focus—although even focussing he still found himself overly absorbed at a scenario he had not once considered.

Would he back off the deal in exchange for that luscious body at his disposal?

Sex and women had never—not once—come ahead of business for him, but in this instance Leo found himself giving serious consideration to breaking that sacred principle.

Angry with himself, he shook his head and looked at her coolly from under lowered lashes. 'You seem to be having a problem accepting the deal I've offered you.'

'Is that why you called me in? To go over all this? Do you think you can intimidate me if there isn't an army of lawyers and accountants around?'

Maddie wanted to sound firm and in control, and she wondered whether he could detect the nervous wobble in her voice.

She'd spent ages wondering when she should break the news of her pregnancy to him. Or even if she should tell him at all! Not only had he been a fleeting visitor in her life but he had entered it under false pretences. Was that the sort of man she wanted as an influence on any child of hers?

He might do crazy things to her body, but wasn't he just another mega-wealthy guy who believed that life was his for the taking? Arrogant? Superior? Not above stamping on other people if it suited them? Hadn't she had too much experience of men like that to invite one into her life simply because she'd happened to fall pregnant by him?

She had had enough of a shock—was now facing enough of an altered future. Did she want to further compound the situation by telling Leo?

Of course there was a chance that he might just shrug and walk away from the whole situation, but what if he didn't?

He would be around *for ever*.

The pros and cons had gone round and round in her head in the space of a handful of hours, but the reality was that she had known from the very second she had seen that pink line that there was no way she could keep the pregnancy from him.

She knew what it felt like to grow up without a father. It was not something she would recommend. Not unless she had very good reason to go down that route.

Her mother had made her choices and Maddie had known that those choices had been difficult and irretrievable. Her own father had been a bastard—a coward and a fortune-hunter.

Leo, whatever else he might be, was none of those things.

So, as she waited to hear what he had to say, for his conversation to play out before hers could begin, she knew that her nerves stemmed from her own revelations to come rather than whatever it was he had summoned her into his office to impart.

'You should have a look at his.' Leo reached towards a slender file and pushed it across the desk to her.

Business was business. That had always been his mantra. Even if she *had* agreed to see him so that she could somehow seduce him into doing what she wanted, there was no way he would succumb to the temptation. At any rate, the defiant tilt of her head was *not* the body language of a woman gearing up to use her feminine wiles on him, and Leo knew that, however pleasurable it had been to play with that tantalising thought, he would have thought a great deal less of her had she chosen to go down that road.

So what choice did he have but to play the cards in his hand?

He watched carefully as she took the file and opened it. He noted the pallor in her cheeks, followed by hot colour as she read and then re-read the report he had received a couple of days ago.

When she'd finished reading it, her head remained lowered, even though she'd quietly closed the file and kept it on her lap.

Deep-seated unease coursed through him, unfamiliar and disconcerting. Leo had no idea what to do with those feelings because he'd never had them before.

This wasn't playing dirty. This information hadn't come into his possession via bribery or blackmail. It was documented, and it had been sourced in five seconds flat by the man he'd instructed.

So why did he now feel like a cad? Why was that lowered head doing all sorts of things to his conscience?

Leo scowled. 'Well?'

'Well, what?' Maddie looked at him. Her eyes were filled with unshed tears. 'Is this why you summoned me to come and see you? I'm surprised you aren't surrounded by your army of lawyers so that they can pick me apart and then spit me out. Because that's why you've got this, isn't it? So that you can use it against me. So that you can force me to sell to you under the threat of making this information public. How *could* you, Leo?'

Leo flushed darkly. 'This information is in the public domain, Maddie.'

'That doesn't mean that you should use it to scare me into doing as you say.'

Suddenly restless, Leo rose to his feet in one easy movement and began pacing his office, finally returning to his desk, perching on the edge of it right in front of her.

'Tell me what happened.'

'Why?' Her green eyes flashed.

'Because I want to hear.'

Leo sighed and raked his fingers through his hair. It felt as though life had been a lot more straightforward before this woman had entered it. Under normal circumstances, with ammunition available, he certainly wouldn't be hanging around asking for back stories.

But he could see that she was trying hard not to cry and that cut him to the quick. The report was simply factual. There would be more to it than was written in black and white.

Maddie glared at him and hesitated. Inside, anger warred with pride. He looked as though he really wanted to hear what she had to say, but how could she trust him? This was the guy who had pretended to be a pauper because it had suited his purpose at the time.

'Please, Maddie.' Leo surprised himself but he meant it. 'What's there is the skeleton of a story. Fill it out for me.'

'How did you know what to look for?'

'I didn't. But I always do very thorough background checks on people and companies before I put money on the table and start signing papers.'

'And if you come across something dodgy you use it against them? Is that it?'

'It's standard business practice to make sure all the facts are on the table. Any fresh-faced accounts manager might have a gambling problem, and that's something that would require close scrutiny of the books. I'm not a big, bad wolf. I'm doing what anyone else would do in my situation.'

Maddie looked down at her fingers and then met his hooded gaze. 'When my mother died,' she began, avoiding sentiment and keeping strictly to the facts, 'I was all over the place. I'd had to abandon my university dreams to look after her, as I think I told you. I therefore left school with a lot of dreams but not much hope of realising any of them, or even of getting a halfway decent job.'

She drew in a deep, steadying breath and detached herself from the remembered emotion. Leo was gazing at her levelly, his expression neither sympathetic nor unsympathetic, merely interested.

'I made money doing menial stuff, and eventually found a well-paid job working for a lovely elderly lady in one of the most expensive suburbs in Sydney. I lived in—which suited me because I saved on rent. In return I took care of her, and I also helped her with an autobiography she was writing. Through her I met Adam, her grandson. He was handsome and charming and... Well, the whole package, really. Or so I thought. We began dating. I was cautious at first. I've had experience with boys wanting to go out with me because of the way...'

She blushed and he looked at her with amusement, as if he'd never heard any woman so obviously wanting to play down her attractiveness.

'Because of the way you look?' he inserted smoothly, and she gave a jerky nod.

'I really thought we had something good,' she said bitterly. 'I really believed that life was being kind to me after all I'd been through with my mum. Anyway, that's by the by.'

She gathered herself, told herself that this wasn't a confessional in front of someone who was going to give her a big bear hug before telling her that everything was going to be all right. This was a story that she wanted to relate because she refused to be defined by the cold, harsh facts without him hearing what was behind those facts.

They might be on opposite sides of the fence now, but they'd also been as intimate as it was possible for two people to get. Something inside her didn't want him to be left with the wrong impression of her.

At which thought, she firmed her soft mouth and ploughed on. 'Lacey—the lady I worked for—started getting forgetful shortly after I started with her. Small things at first, and I didn't think anything of it. Not enough for alarm bells to start ringing. But then it seemed to progress quite fast—although it's possible that I just didn't notice anything to begin with because I was in recovery from Mum's death.'

She sneaked a glance at him. Was he bored? Maybe trying to sift through the information so that he could find her weak spot? She recalled what his PA had said about him being fair and realised that, however angry she was with him, she *did* think that he was fair.

'And then?' But Leo had some idea of what was going to come, and he knew that it would all be wrapped up with the ex she had fled from.

'A very valuable necklace went missing. It was worth…well, more than I can say. Adam and his sister blamed me. I tried to tell them… I couldn't believe that the guy I'd thought I had a future with could turn on me—could believe that I was nothing more than a common thief and a liar.'

She broke eye contact and stared without blinking for a few seconds, gathering herself.

Angry at a man he'd never met in his life, and held captive by the strangest surge of protectiveness, Leo thrust a box of tissues from his drawer towards her. She snatched a few without tearing her eyes away from the wall.

She sucked in some air and crumpled the tissues in her hand, then looked at Leo levelly.

'No one believed me,' she said simply, 'and Lacey was so forgetful that no one took much notice of her at all. There was a missing necklace, and I was a poor girl from the wrong side of the tracks, so therefore there was no question that I was guilty. The police were called in and I was formally charged with theft.

'I was staring a prison sentence in the face, or at least the threat of one, when one of the police officers, having chatted to Lacey, brought in a medic. She was diagnosed with Alzheimer's. Shortly after that, by a stroke of luck, the necklace resurfaced. It had been in the pocket of one of her skirts. She must have removed it and stuck it in there when she was out in the garden. I was unconditionally cleared of all charges—but mud sticks and all I wanted to do was run away. The whole episode... I felt dirty, disgraced, even though I'd done nothing wrong. The questions...the suspicions...and then the horror of what could have happened if that diagnosis hadn't been made—if one person hadn't noticed what no one else had... It was all too much.'

She laughed shortly.

'So you were right when you said that I must have been running away from something.'

'And the ex?'

'What about him?'

'Did he come crawling back to apologise, clutching flowers and the engagement ring you were hoping he would eventually put on your finger?'

Maddie stiffened with pride. 'I broke off all contact with his entire family and with him. He got the message loud and clear that I wanted nothing more to do with him.'

'But he hurt you?'

'What do you think?'

'Then suddenly, out of the blue, you discover that you're the sole beneficiary of old Tommaso's dwindling fortune…'

'It's my chance to do something with my life, to move on, and I'm going to take it.'

Did she mean that even now that circumstances had changed? Leo had detected the shadow of a hesitation in that declaration. She said she wasn't going to cave in and sell to him. She'd shouted that from the rooftops. But there was an inflection in her voice that made him wonder just how adamant she was about that.

He'd increased his offer. The diminutive lawyer who had traipsed along in her wake must have opened her eyes to the advantages of taking what had been put on the table.

He looked at the folder, still resting on her lap, his dark eyes lazy, thoughtful, speculative.

Maddie followed that lazy gaze. It didn't take a genius to figure out that he knew just what he had to do to get her where he wanted her. She'd been exonerated of all charges, her name fully cleared, but any brush with the law would be enough to have bankers and shareholders running to the table to snatch at the deal Leo had thrown down—even if she *had* emerged as pure as driven snow from the unfortunate episode.

'You're going to use this information against me, aren't you?' she said quietly.

Leo, who had decided to do no such thing, allowed a telling silence to develop between them.

'Do you think it would be fair for all parties involved in this deal—all the people who stand to gain or lose by the decision you and I make—that they remain in ignorance of what's taken place?'

It was a valid enough question as far as Leo was concerned, even though he knew without a shadow of a doubt, as he watched the emotions flicker across her beautiful face, that he would bury the report—bury it so well that it would never see the light of day.

'I see.' Maddie stood up. 'I wonder why I expected anything different.'

'Sit down!'

'Don't you *dare* tell me what to do! I should have guessed that all rich men are exactly the same. They may talk differently and walk differently, but in the end they're all the same. They're all prepared to go the extra mile when it comes to getting what they want.'

'That is outrageous!'

'Is it? Okay, Leo, you win. I'll take whatever deal it is you want to offer. I'll accept the money and I'll go away—because the last thing I need is to start a new life over here with my past following behind me like a bad smell!'

'Stop being hysterical and *sit down*! Whoever said anything about my using this information? I admit under normal circumstances I wouldn't hesitate, but in this instance...'

Maddie barely heard a word he was saying. Her heart was beating as fast and as hard as a sledgehammer and she was breathing so rapidly that she thought she might hyperventilate.

Which was the last thing she needed in her condition.

And suddenly the whole point of this meeting surged back to her consciousness and she stared at him.

'Are you going to sit down?' Leo demanded, vaulting upright and swinging round his desk so that he was staring down at her. 'And before we go any further let's get one thing straight—I am *nothing* like that scumbag you got mixed up with! I don't lead women up any garden paths and I damn well would *never* shout guilty until proved innocent!'

'But you *would* drag my name through the mud even though I *am* innocent!'

'Have you heard *a word* I've said to you?'

Maddie stared fiercely at him. Without even realising what she was doing, she rested the flat of her hand against his chest, warding him off but wanting badly to draw him towards her.

She sprang away, shocked at how he could scramble her brains even when she was in the midst of a ferocious argument.

'I am *not* going to use any information against you, Maddie, so you can relax on that score. It doesn't mean that I won't get the store from you, because I will, but I won't be making any of this sorry business public knowledge in order to further my intentions.'

Maddie stared. Her hand still burned from where she had rested it against his chest. *She was turned on by him.* There was no ignoring the hot dampness between her thighs and the pinching of her nipples.

Maybe it was her hormones, she thought wildly. Her responses were going every which way. She had come here planning on being cool and contained, but very quickly all those good intentions had unravelled and now here she was, screaming at him and not listening to a word he was saying.

He wasn't going to use the information he had uncovered. That didn't matter, however. This meeting had disclosed something very important—something she couldn't just look away from in the hope that she might be wrong.

She still wanted Leo more than she'd ever wanted anything or anyone in her life before.

No matter what she thought of him personally, her body still craved his touch and that terrified her.

So the fighting would end.

She would hand over the store to him and she would tell him about the baby.

But once the store was his, contact would be effectively broken. She would take the money and she would sell her grandfather's house and leave Ireland for good.

Maddie didn't think that a fully paid up member of the successful bachelor club would travel far and wide to see a child he had never committed to having in the first place. She would be able to step back from something that felt a lot like fire. The life she would build would not hold the legacy she had inherited, but it would have something else—something equally important. A child. Plus, she would have more than enough money to support them both.

'You don't have to fight me for the store, Leo. I told you. It's yours for the taking. You can get your lawyers to talk to Anthony and they can sort out the sale.'

Leo took a step back and tilted his head to one side, as though listening for a noise he couldn't quite hear. Yet.

'And your change of heart stems from…?'

Maddie backed towards the door until she was pressed against it. 'I have more on my plate now than just the store.'

'Explain.' Leo took two steps towards her, the depth of his navy eyes skewering her temporarily to the spot.

'I'm pregnant, Leo.'

She stared at him and watched the colour drain away from his face. He was a man who'd been slammed by a train at full speed and was finding it hard to breathe.

The outer office was empty. Maddie could tell that much. She realised Leo must have dismissed the PA, knowing that his chat with her was going to be highly personal, involving sensitive information about her past.

'I don't believe you.'

'I'm pregnant. So you can have the damned store! I'm going now. I'll give you a chance to digest what I've said. But the store is yours and that's the main thing. Isn't it?'

With which parting shot she pulled open the door and shot out of his office, walking briskly without a backward glance towards the elevator that had earlier whooshed her up to his office.

CHAPTER SIX

MADDIE DIDN'T MAKE IT. Not quite. As he followed her into the elevator she spun round, the look on her face evidence that she hadn't heard him behind her.

'Leo…'

'You don't get to do this, Maddie.'

'Do what?'

'Detonate a bomb in my life and then make a run for it.'

'I wasn't making a run for it.'

'We're going back to my apartment and you're going to tell me in words of one syllable what the hell is going on!'

But Leo knew what was going on. He'd taken an appalling chance and now the chickens had come home to roost. She wasn't lying. She wasn't the sort. He was going to be a father, and it was a nightmare so all-encompassing that he had to absorb it in stages.

After all the lessons he'd learnt from the five-second marriage that should never have happened, and which had ended up costing him an arm and a leg and certainly a great deal of pride, he'd blithely had unprotected sex with a woman because he hadn't been able to resist.

After a decade of playing it safe, never taking

chances and avoiding anything that smelled like a honey trap, he'd blown it all with a woman he'd known for less than a day.

But, by God, the sex had been amazing.

Leo was infuriated that that ridiculous thought had the nerve even to cross his mind when what he had to deal with was the fact that life as he knew it was over.

He wondered, briefly, whether she had engineered the whole bloody mess—but that suspicion barely lasted a second. Somehow, however cynical he was on the subject of women and what they would do when it came to getting their hands on pots of gold, there was something fundamentally honest about Maddie.

His mouth twisted as he followed that thought through to its logical conclusion.

She was bone-deep honest, and while he would happily have said the same for himself—despite his ruthlessness when it came to business dealings—he knew that she distrusted him. He'd ferreted out information about her, and even though he'd told her that he wasn't going to use it, the fact that it was out there, in his possession, had awakened that distrust of him.

Added to that was the small technicality of him keeping his true identity under wraps when they'd first met, and it was little wonder that she was desperate to find the nearest exit.

Tough.

He hadn't banked on this, but he wasn't a man who dodged any bullet.

He looked at her with brooding intensity. Never had he felt so restless, and yet, confined in their ten-by-ten metal box, he had no choice but to deal with the riptide of emotions flooding through him without moving a muscle.

She was keeping her eyes studiously averted. She looked as though she would break in two if he so much as reached out and touched her.

'I'm not going to your apartment with you,' Maddie said as the elevator doors opened, disgorging them back into the foyer where she had sat earlier, awash with nerves.

'Well, sorry to be a party-pooper, but if you think you're escaping back to Dublin before we can talk about this…this…*situation* then you've got another think coming.'

'You need time to mull it over,' she said, and her voice held an urgent, panicky undertone. 'You need time to digest.'

Leo didn't bother to dignify that suggestion with an answer. Walking out of the building, he was simultaneously calling his driver and keeping an extremely watchful eye on the bombshell dragging her feet alongside him. If she was searching for the most effective way of vanishing, then she was out of luck.

To his satisfaction, he saw that James, on the ball as always, was pulling to a stop in the black Jag. Leo opened the back door and propelled Maddie in without skipping a beat.

Maddie barely knew what was happening. One minute she was racking her brains to try and think of a way of avoiding Leo and his crazy suggestion that they go to his apartment to talk, and the next minute she was somehow in the back seat of a car, which was being driven by a young man with curly dark hair and lots of gold jewellery.

She was almost distracted enough by the sight to forget *why* she was in the back seat of Leo's car. Then it slammed back into her with force and she turned to him and hissed, 'You can't do this. You can't just… just…*kidnap me*…'

'Kidnap you? Stop over-dramatising, Maddie. And instead of wasting your energy trying to fight me, just accept that I intend to have this conversation you're obviously desperate to avoid.'

'I'm not *desperate* to avoid anything! I just thought that you might need time to…to…'

'Get to grips with the grenade you've just detonated in my life?'

Maddie looked at him furiously. Conscious of the strange driver at the wheel, Maddie resorted to resentful silence—which Leo did not attempt to break.

She wished she could read what was going on in his head. What was he thinking? She'd imagined that when she broke the news he would be furious. Shocked to start with, but then furious.

She had pictured herself backing out of his office, leaving him to plot how he could get rid of her and a baby he hadn't asked for as quietly and efficiently as possible. She hadn't envisaged a scenario in which she was being driven to his apartment.

In silence.

The drive took half an hour, and then she was treated to the splendour of London at its finest as the car pulled up outside a redbrick Victorian mansion, with very precise black railings and a row of perfectly groomed shaped shrubs edging the shallow bank of steps that led up to a pristine black door.

It turned out that his penthouse apartment ranged

across the top two floors. In a daze, she followed him into a wide, ornate hallway, where a porter made sure uninvited riff-raff were kept out, into a mirrored lift and then straight up into his apartment.

The lift was obviously for his use only.

Inside, greys and creams blended with wood and dull chrome. On the walls, impressive abstract art provided splashes of colour. It was all very open-plan, and configured in such a way that the most was made of the soaring ceilings and the two floors were connected by a glass and iron staircase.

Leo was walking towards a sitting area dominated by two oversized white leather sofas and Maddie followed him.

'When did you find out?' he asked without preamble. 'And there's no point perching on the edge of the sofa as though you're about to turn tail and run. You won't be going anywhere until we've discussed this... this...nightmare.'

'It's not a *nightmare*...'

'Well, it's certainly not a dream come true. When did you find out?'

'Yesterday.'

'And your plan was to show up in my office, hand me the keys to the store, inform me that you were carrying my child and then what? Head for the hills? Disappear under cover of darkness?'

Maddie reddened because, roughly speaking, he wasn't too far from the truth.

Eyes narrowed, Leo said coolly. 'It's not going to happen.'

'Which part?' Maddie asked faintly.

'The trade-off. I get the store, you get to run away. *Not* going to happen.'

'Leo…' Maddie breathed in deeply. 'We had a few hours of fun. Neither of us planned on having to deal with any consequences…'

A few hours of fun? Leo was inexplicably outraged to hear himself dismissed as *a few hours of fun*. He knew, rationally, that this was exactly how *he* would have categorised most of his exploits with women. Maybe slightly more than just the few hours, but essentially the same sentiment. Fun on the run.

That didn't make it any more acceptable.

'You didn't bank on my getting pregnant,' Maddie said, ignoring his glowering expression and ploughing on, 'and I get it that you're a bachelor through and through. The last thing you need or want is the sort of lifelong commitment that a child brings—especially when you didn't ask for this situation. No one wants to find that their nicely ordered perfect life has suddenly turned into a *nightmare.*'

Leo knew that she made sense. He was a committed bachelor. She wasn't to know why that was so deeply ingrained in him, but she had hit the nail on the head anyway. She had also been right when she'd said that the last thing he'd ever have asked for would be the lifelong commitment of a child—a duty of care stretching into infinity.

'I *didn't* ask for this,' he grated, 'but I'm honest enough to admit that no one held a gun to my head and forced me into having unprotected sex with you.'

'It doesn't matter. It's happened, and I'm not going to be responsible for lumbering you with a burden you didn't ask for.' She angled her head stubbornly and firmed her mouth. 'Well?' she pressed into the silence between them. 'You're not saying anything,'

'I'm waiting for you to finish what *you* want to say.'

Maddie breathed out a sigh. 'That's good.'

She cleared her throat to move on to stage two of the speech she had prepared in her head. It was a rough outline of the only solution she could think of, bearing in mind that she, herself, was still coming to terms with the fundamental change to her life looming on the not too distant horizon.

'If I sell the store to you then I will have more than sufficient money to make a life for myself and the baby. You won't have to take on any lifelong financial commitment. In fact you won't have to take on any commitment at all. In this day and age, single parent families are the norm.'

'I'm touched by your thoughtfulness and generosity,' Leo drawled. 'I can't think of a single other woman who, given the same circumstances, would be so overjoyed to see me walk scot-free.'

'Well…'

'Maybe it's because of your father.'

'What do you mean?'

'The stupendously low opinion you have of men.'

Maddie reddened. 'I'm giving you the option of not having your life ruined—'

'That's a very emotive word. *Ruined.*'

'So is *nightmare*,' Maddie countered, without batting an eye.

'Well, we won't be using either, because I won't be walking away scot-free. You're assuming that I'm the type of guy who's so self-interested that he's happy to get a woman pregnant and then leave her in the lurch.'

Maddie stiffened. 'What are you saying?'

'I may not have asked for this situation, but now that it's arisen walking away from it isn't going to be the solution I'll be taking.'

'You want the store.'

'It's bricks and mortar. I'm prepared to put that particular want on the back burner.'

'But I can't handle the responsibility of turning the place around when I'm going to have to deal with pregnancy and a newborn!'

'You can't handle it *alone*…'

'Even with help from a team of managers and workers…'

'Of course we'll have to discuss what the way forward with the store should be,' Leo mused, rising to his feet in one lithe, graceful movement to stroll towards the high-tech open-plan kitchen, where he proceeded to get them both something cold to drink.

Bewildered, Maddie twisted round to follow him. The accoutrements of a businessman had been shed along his way. The sleeves of his shirt were rolled to the elbow, and she hadn't noticed but he had slipped off his leather shoes and socks and was barefoot. He looked so stunning, so sophisticated…*so completely out of her league*.

She thought of Adam and her foolishness in falling for someone else who had been out of her league. She thought of the way he had stood back, siding with his family, accusing her of theft and not caring that her whole life was unravelling.

She thought of Leo, accessing that private information. Even if he had decided to withhold using it against her she knew that he would have considered that option because that was the kind of man that he was.

She didn't know what was going on, but she felt a shiver of apprehension slither down her spine.

'Leo, I have no idea what you're talking about,' she confessed, having accepted the mineral water he had poured for her only to place it on the glass coffee table next to her.

'Don't you?'

'*What* way forward with the store?'

'Like I mentioned to you before, the day of the dinosaur department store, jack of all trades and master of none, is coming to an end.'

He was covering the room in ever-diminishing circles and finally he was standing directly in front of her, navy eyes unreadable, oozing just the sort of unfair sex appeal that made a nonsense of her attempts to get her brain in working order.

Maddie frowned. 'I don't know where you're going with this. Yes, I would have loved to have held on to the store, kept it as it was, but if you have it then what you do with it is no longer my concern.'

'You haven't *listened* to me, have you, Maddie?'

'I…'

'I'm not buying the store. Neither am I going anywhere. You're pregnant, and this completely changes the basis of our relationship.'

'But, Leo, we don't *have* a relationship.'

'You're the mother of my unborn baby. What do you call *that*?'

Faced with this direct question, which seemed to beg a sensible answer she was struggling to provide, Maddie could only stare at him speechlessly.

'Believe me,' Leo said heavily, moving to sit on the chair adjacent to her, stretching out his long legs at an angle and then relaxing back with his fingers linked on his stomach. 'I hadn't banked on any of this happening. But happen it has, and as far as I can see there's only one sensible solution that's going to work. I will have to marry you and legitimise my child.'

Maddie's mouth fell open. Before she could say anything he held up one assured hand, as though to stop her before she could interrupt. Which she wasn't about to do because her vocal cords had seized up.

'I won't lie to you, Maddie, marriage has not been on my radar. I'm a red-blooded male and I've had my fun, but I haven't been tempted to turn fun into anything more serious. You have your past, and that's shaped you. I have mine.'

'What? What past? This is exactly what I'm talking about. I don't know anything about you! How can you sit there and start talking about marriage when we don't know one another? It's crazy.'

'Crazy it may be, but we're in the most intimate situation it's possible for two people to be in.'

'And, as you've just said, you've never considered marriage! So how on earth do you expect me to react when you sit there now, telling me that's the only solution to this situation?'

'You're looking at this in the wrong way—putting an unnecessarily negative spin on it.'

'What do you mean?'

'Marriage in the conventional sense of the word isn't something I believe in, and there's no point in my pretending otherwise.'

'"The conventional sense of the word"? Would that

be the convention of two people being together because they're in love?'

'The world is littered with kids who end up in therapy because of parents who got married because they thought they were *in love*. Your mother,' he inserted shrewdly, 'thought *she* was in love, and absconded to the other side of the world in complete defiance of common sense only for the marriage to end in tears.'

Maddie flushed. 'That's not the point.'

'It's precisely the point. You had all contact with this country and your grandfather severed because of your mother's headstrong pursuit of *love*.'

Maddie didn't answer because he had a point. 'You're twisting everything to suit your argument,' she muttered, shooting him a fulminating look from under her lashes. 'I didn't see this side of you when we…when I…'

'When you were overwhelmed with lust and jumped into bed with me?'

'You're *so* arrogant. I should have known that you couldn't be a carefree wanderer. Someone like that would have been a lot more humble, a lot more down-to-earth. He wouldn't have had an ego the size of a cruise liner.'

Leo grinned, because in spite of the tenseness of the situation he was enjoying her dry sense of humour and the way she wasn't caving in to him. *Yet*.

'One of those humble, down-to-earth, carefree wandering souls would have hit the high seas the minute you told him you were pregnant. Generally speaking, perpetual Peter Pans don't cope well with the thought of being tied down. Which brings us back to the matter in hand. What I'm proposing is a union for the sake of our child. A practical solution. Something that makes sense.'

'Oh, wow, Leo. You're *really* selling it to me,' Maddie said acidly. 'I always dreamed of love and marriage and then the pitter-patter of tiny feet. Now you're presenting me with marriage, the pitter-patter of tiny feet, and forget about love because love doesn't count for anything.'

'You thought you'd found love with a loser who turned on you because he thought you were a thief. So much for the myth that love can survive through thick and thin. Convince me that love is all that matters when your mother learnt the hard way and so did you. Love is all a crock of—'

'Stop!' Maddie stood up to pace the room. 'Look…' She breathed in deeply. 'I know you mean well, and you have good intentions, and your offer is very generous, but I can't think of anything worse than being stuck with someone with whom I have no emotional connection.'

Stuck with? Was she actually *trying* to enrage him?

'But this isn't about *you,* is it?'

'Not entirely.' Maddie reddened. 'But it's not all about our child either. Yes, every child deserves two parents—but only if those parents are happy and committed to one another.'

Leo could no longer contain his impatience. 'Strip back the jargon and how many couples tick all the boxes?' Restless, he stood up to prowl the room, just as she was, until they were facing one another like opponents in a ring.

'I don't care about how many couples tick the boxes or don't,' Maddie muttered stubbornly, tearing her eyes away from his ridiculously beautiful face. 'I care about whether *I* would be able to tick the boxes with my partner.'

'Oh, bring on the violin music!' Leo fought down the urge to thump something in sheer frustration. How was it that he was having to wage war in an effort to persuade someone to share a life of obscene wealth and privilege?

'I couldn't bear the thought of being married to someone because he felt responsible for a situation he hadn't banked on.'

'Are you telling me that you would rather jeopardise the well-being of a child for your own selfish concerns?'

'It's not selfish.'

'You of all people should be able to understand the limitations of a life with only one parent. Yes, it's common. Yes, single parent families are a statistic. But you are turning down the option of *two* parents. Do you think our child will thank you for that in the years to come?'

Maddie glared, buffeted by the pull of his arguments, all of which made perfect sense in a way, but…

'We don't *love* one another,' she cried in protest.

She thought of those moments they'd shared and was embarrassed at how powerful her instinct was to read into them a bonding and a meeting of minds that hadn't been there. There had been something about that brief time they'd spent together that had made her feel as though she'd found her soulmate.

'What happens when we get bored with one another? What happens when you start resenting the fact that you're tied to someone you don't want to be with?'

'I don't see the point of conjecture. We have to deal with the here and now.'

'How can you be so...*practical*?'

'Because one of us needs to be.'

'I can't marry you. Yes, I *know* I should be hardened and cynical—but I'm not.'

Leo could recognise defeat as well as the next man. He'd approached the situation from the only perspective that made sense and had automatically assumed that she would fall in line—because, frankly, what woman wouldn't? He'd failed to take into account the fact that it was fair to say in the short space of time he'd known her she had been nothing like any of the women he had ever gone out with. So why should she react with any degree of predictability?

Too late he was recognising that she was as headstrong and stubborn as a mule, and as capable of digging her heels in as strenuously as he was.

'Are you telling me that you'd like to spread your net and see what you can catch while you're pregnant with my baby?'

'Of course not! What man is going to look twice at a woman who's having someone else's child?'

'You'd be shocked,' he muttered in a driven undertone.

When he thought of her putting herself out there, finding some loser who was only interested in spinning her some line so that he could crawl all over her body, he saw red. But he was quick enough to realise that any show of anger wasn't going to cut it. The more he tried to cajole and badger her into seeing things from his point of view, the more she was going to backpedal and see him as the bad guy, trying to force her into a loathsome life of undiluted luxury.

'Okay.' He held his hand up in a gesture of surrender

that made Maddie narrow her eyes suspiciously. 'Let's move on to another pragmatic approach to the situation. One that excludes what I still maintain is the most desirable solution. You don't want marriage? Well, I can't frogmarch you up the aisle, bound and tied. But we're going to have to approach this calmly.'

He patted the space on the sofa next to him and she sat down and twisted to look at him.

His dark, dark blue eyes immediately made Maddie feel hot and bothered, but when she looked away all she could see was the taut pull of his trousers over his muscular thighs, the bronzed forearms liberally sprinkled with dark hair, the way that dark hair curled round the matt gold of his watch strap... She felt faint.

'Go on,' she managed to croak, noting that he had dumped the marriage solution faster than the speed of light when she'd provided him with a get-out clause.

'I will want to be actively involved in everything from this point onwards. And I certainly will not risk you doing a runner by buying the store from you. You want it. It's yours. That way I am assured that you won't be leaving the place any time soon.'

'But you live here...in London...'

'And naturally I'll continue to oversee things here. But I can run my empire from anywhere in the world, such is the nature of communications these days. And Dublin seems to be an extremely charming place in which to settle... Nice restaurants, spectacular scenery, friendly locals...'

Leo thought that he could usefully live there for a few months and use that time to source an alternative location for his business... Or he might just explore the outskirts of the city and put in place the makings of a golf complex which he had been toying with for some time. It would be a little holiday, in a manner of speaking.

Naturally his grandfather would be curious as to his sudden change of location from London to Dublin, and the absence of a deal on the store, and in due course Leo would explain all. If Maddie was wary of *him*, then being confronted by his grandfather, whose thoughts about children being born out of wedlock were firmly rooted somewhere in the Victorian era, would have her running for the hills.

And, up close and personal, he would be able to keep an eye on her. She had dug her heels in and refused the marriage solution, but there was more than one way to skin a cat, and Leo was in little doubt that she would see the wisdom of that solution once she began to struggle with the technicalities of running a store…when the difficulties of being a single parent loomed all the more glaringly.

Because he would be there right next to her—a constant alternative waiting in the wings. He would get the girl, he thought, even if he had to play the waiting game for a bit.

'But you don't… You don't have anywhere to live here…'

Maddie wondered what it would be like to live with him, to wake up next to him every morning and go to sleep with the warmth of his body against hers. And then she immediately killed that stupid fantasy, because nothing could be further from reality.

This was never going to be a love story with a happy ending.

'That won't be a problem.' Leo shrugged. 'I'll buy somewhere.'

'*Buy* somewhere?'

'You'd be surprised how fast a house can change hands when enough money is put on the table,' Leo said drily. 'I don't foresee a problem.'

'I won't do a runner. How can I when I'll have a store to oversee? There's no need for you to decamp to Ireland.'

Leo spread his arms wide in a gesture of magnanimity which made her think of a predatory shark, trying to convince a school of minnows that, no, it wasn't *in the least bit* interested in gobbling them up.

'Like I said, whether you do a runner or not, I intend to be here for you every step of the way.' He shot her a slow, curling smile. 'You'll have me around twenty-four-seven—without the inconvenience of a wedding ring on your finger...'

CHAPTER SEVEN

MADDIE LOOKED AT the half-finished building work which she had tentatively begun on her house six weeks previously. It was just another aggravating headache added to the pile of aggravating headaches which had been slowly but steadily mounting ever since she had confidently declared to Leo that if he didn't want to buy the store from her then she was overjoyed, because she would be able to rebuild her family's legacy and return it to its former glory.

Niggling problems had arisen at the store. Missing stock, inadequate paperwork for suppliers which had only just come to light, a persistent leak in one of the departments on the top floor, which the plumbing team had ominously told her *'looked bad'*... After that she had dismissed them, so that she could consider her options.

Several members of staff had also chosen to quit, following the announcement of her ownership, and replacing them was proving another headache because everyone seemed to think that there was no chance the store was a viable employer—even though she had personally sat in at all the interviews and done her best to persuade them otherwise.

And now this.

Maddie sighed and contemplated the exposed plasterboard and the flooring which had been ripped up—but not in its entirety. Which meant that half the kitchen floor was comprised of the original tired tiles and the other half of bare brick and wood, with enough gaps to let in several families of rodents.

The fridge had been disconnected, and now the builder had phoned to say that he wasn't going to be around for the next week because of a 'personal emergency'.

Maddie looked at her phone.

Leo.

She didn't want to think of him but she did. She couldn't help herself. True to his word, he had been around a lot. Phoning her. Arranging to meet her for lunch. Insisting on doing the occasional grocery shop with her because he wanted to make sure she was buying food that was nutritious.

She refused to invite him back to her house, just as she discouraged his visits to the store. She wanted and needed her independence. She'd turned him down and for good reason. The last thing she wanted was to drift into a state where she found herself depending on him, and she knew that was a real danger because he was just so damned *present*. The perfect gentleman.

There had been no mention of marriage, nothing that could be construed as being remotely sexual... He was just strong, reliable, and annoyingly, infuriatingly *helpful*.

Maddie knew that she should be grateful that he'd never overstepped the mark.

She didn't want him in the house? He shrugged and took the hint with alacrity.

She was vague about him visiting the store? He acquiesced with another of those non-committal shrugs of his.

He treated her as though she was made of porcelain, and the only time she'd sensed that he was having trouble backing down was when she had absolutely refused to see his private doctor on a weekly basis because it was 'better safe than sorry'.

All in all, he had treated her with tact, consideration and a detached courtesy. And, however much she told herself that that was a *good* thing, she hated it.

On the spur of the moment she dialled the hotline number. For the first time since he had given it to her weeks ago.

In the middle of a high-level meeting, attended by a select handful of people who had come to see him because he had no intention of spreading himself thin by going to see *them*, Leo raised one imperious hand, at which all conversation stopped.

Maddie's name had flashed up on his screen, and since it was the first time she had deigned to call him he had no intention of ignoring the call.

Frankly, he'd grown tired of waiting. To start with he'd expected her to phone him within a few days—if only because *he* called *her* with tiresome regularity, and whatever had happened to good manners and meeting halfway on the effort front?

Then, when no phone call had materialised, he'd banked on that changing just as soon as she'd unearthed all the problems at the store. Hadn't he volunteered to help her often enough?

Several weeks later and he'd all but given up.

'Leo,' he said now, without preamble.

'Sorry, I'm disturbing you,' Maddie apologised, the reluctance in her voice making it clear how uncomfortable she was having given in to the temptation of calling him.

Leo looked at the room full of important people who had gathered there for his convenience. 'Not in the slightest.'

'It's just that…'

'Tell me what's wrong.' He half turned, making a motion with one hand to inform the gathering that they were to continue without him and indicating that his second-in-command would host.

'Nothing's wrong… It's just that…well… I'm here at home…' Maddie gazed with despair at the half-finished kitchen, in which cooking no halfway decent meal had been possible for the past two weeks. 'And I'm having one or two little problems… It's nothing, really… I shouldn't have bothered you.'

'I'm on my way.'

Leo killed the phone call before she could launch into a long-winded monologue of apology.

For the first time in his life he knew what it felt like to be worried. He was worried now. He'd never met anyone as stubbornly determined to be self-sufficient as Maddie, and the fact that she had confessed to having 'one or two problems' was a source of high-voltage concern—because *'one or two problems'* could range from a chipped nail to the sky falling down.

No, he thought, scrap the chipped nail and go straight to the sky falling down.

His Ferrari was equipped to deliver him to her house in record time, and he rang the doorbell and kept his finger there, already planning on breaking the door down if she didn't answer it within ten seconds.

She answered it before brute force became necessary.

'What's wrong?' were his opening words as he strode past her into the hall and then spun round on his heel, eyes narrowed, inspecting her from head to toe for visible signs of distress.

She was as stunning as she always was. Very slightly showing her pregnancy now, but it was hardly noticeable under the jogging bottoms and the baggy top.

Distractedly, Leo marvelled that she could take the most unfortunate of outfits and turn it into something intensely sexy.

He shifted impatiently as his body began to undermine his common sense. As it was wont to do with predictable regularity. She'd laid down her parameters six weeks ago—turned his marriage proposal down and all but said that she deserved someone better than him, someone more suitable, someone who came with the full package.

Forced into a corner, and obliged to bide his time, Leo knew that he couldn't risk undermining his own objectives by giving in to the temptation to put that will power of hers to the test.

He focused on her face, but there was no reprieve there because the connection that lured him in wasn't just about the way she looked or the way his body reacted to hers. Something ran deeper, like a powerful underwater current, and that pull operated on a completely different level.

Leo frowned, as he always did when this kind of thinking ambushed him, not quite knowing what to do with the confused jumble of feelings he couldn't seem to pin down and box up. He spoke to her on the phone and her voice did something to him. It was bizarre, a little perplexing. He didn't care to dwell on it.

Instead, he thought about those sidelong glances when she'd thought he wasn't looking. He could have done something about that, but he'd backed away. Push her even a little at the wrong time, he'd reasoned, and she would be off. And he wasn't going to risk that happening just for the sake of staunching the painful ache of desire that took him over whenever he was around her.

For someone as accustomed as he was to the transitory nature of lust, Leo was a little shocked at how much he still wanted to touch Maddie. Even when she wasn't around she was in his head like a burr. Was it because she had been elevated to a position never previously occupied by any other woman? Mother of his unborn baby. Or was it because the physical side of their relationship had not been allowed to follow its natural course and wind down to its inevitable conclusion?

Maybe it was a mixture of both. Leo didn't know. He just knew that he seemed to be engaged in a permanent battle to keep his hands off her.

Maddie chewed her lip—and then she did the absolute unthinkable. She burst into tears.

Panicked, Leo pulled her to him and held her close. He smoothed her hair and mumbled softly. Just when he needed a handkerchief he discovered that he didn't have one, so he wiped her cheek with his knuckle and listened to her tell him that nothing was wrong, that she didn't know why she was crying and that it could only be hormones—and actually she shouldn't have called him.

'Talk to me,' was his response to all that.

'I feel overwhelmed,' Maddie confessed in a small voice, getting her crazy crying jag under control but not pulling out of his embrace 'The store… The house…'

Since Leo had only heard about developments at the store second-hand, and hadn't been to the house at all, he took a chance to look around him, then beyond her, to the open door through which he glimpsed the chaos of what remained of the kitchen.

Swearing softly under his breath, he edged her away from him. 'Why didn't you tell me?'

He wanted to sweep her off her feet and carry her to the scene of the crime, but rather than spook her with caveman antics he shuffled, still holding her, until they were both in the kitchen. He settled her into one of the chairs that hadn't been rehomed somewhere else while work was being carried out.

Or not, judging from the state of things.

He inspected the shoddy, half-finished mess.

An unusable kitchen.

Leo looked around for another chair and then, not finding one handy, did the caveman thing after all and swept her off her feet as though she weighed nothing. He carried her into the living room, which contained most of the displaced contents of the kitchen.

'I repeat,' he said, gently depositing her on the sofa and then dragging a chair over so that he could pin her to the spot without any room for manoeuvre, 'why didn't you tell me about this sooner?'

'They said it would only take two weeks.'

'Name of the company?'

'Well…'

'Maddie, just tell me who you employed to do this job.'

She fumbled with her cell phone and passed it to him, so that he could see the details of the company she'd used, and then, silencing her with one hand while he phoned them, she listened as he let rip.

No shouting, no bellowing and no threats. His voice was soft—dangerously soft—and the threat was implicit. 'One week,' he said, 'and don't make me regret giving you that long…'

And then he made her tell him, leaving nothing out, what was going on both in the store and the rest of the house.

The store would come together. At least he had a foothold of sorts there, and could make sure no disasters occurred. The house, on the other hand…

'The kitchen is effectively out of bounds?' he said finally, and Maddie nodded sheepishly.

'So how have you been able to eat?'

'I… Well…'

'You're pregnant, Maddie. I don't want to hear any evasive non-answers. Yes, I have taken you out for dinners and the occasional lunch, but in between… Tell me what your diet has been. Because from the looks of it there have been no cooking facilities here for some time.'

Leo had never thought that being the Great Protector could feel so good.

'A little over two weeks…'

'That's plenty long enough when you're supposed to be putting nutrients into your body.'

'I've been eating,' she mumbled sheepishly, but he read in her eyes that it had been a long time since she had seen a homecooked meal.

'This isn't going to do,' Leo said flatly. 'I can't stop you jeopardising your *own* well-being by living off preservative-stuffed junk food, but I *can* and *will* prevent you from damaging the baby you're carrying!'

She pulled herself together and said primly, 'Once everything's in place my eating habits will return to normal. I love cooking. I would never not eat, and you don't have to tell me that this isn't a good time to have an erratic diet. I'm not an idiot.'

'Again, you should have told me sooner.'

'I didn't think the builders would just up and disappear.'

'You're stressed, and stress is the last thing you need right now.'

And, he thought, she couldn't accuse *him* of contributing to the source of her stress, considering he had done nothing but kick his heels for the past few weeks, gritting his teeth in silent frustration as she became more and more entrenched in her determination to prove how self-sufficient she was.

There were times when she seriously made him want to tear his hair out.

'Let's go upstairs,' he said abruptly, coming to a decision and not giving himself time to have any rethink.

Maddie's eyes widened. 'For what?'

Leo looked at her in silence for a few seconds. 'What

would you like it to be for?' he couldn't resist asking, his voice as soft as silk.

He lowered his eyes, annoyed with himself and with the prompt response of his libido to the thought of having her. More than anything he would like to see her changing body...ripening with his child.

'You're going to pack your bags,' he said gruffly, 'because you're leaving here today. With me.'

'What?'

'You recall I mentioned that my grandfather is cruising in the Caribbean and had stopped off to stay on one of the smaller islands? Well, the villa on that island belongs to me, and I intend on taking you there. Unfortunately there will be no meet-and-greet with him, as he's now enjoying the splendours of the open seas, but it's a great place to unwind—and you need to unwind.'

Leo couldn't disguise a certain amount of relief that Benito had left the island. In due course he would meet the woman who would become his future granddaughter-in-law, as far as he was concerned, and Leo hadn't disillusioned him. It was a bridge to be crossed when he got to it. But he would certainly be thrilled to think that they would be going to the villa together—as a couple.

'Leo, that's ridiculous! I can't just...just leave for a holiday while everything here is in disarray!'

But the thought of doing that dangled like a carrot in front of her.

'Leave everything to me,' Leo said, rising to his feet and heading out towards the hall and the staircase while Maddie shot up and tripped along behind him.

'I can manage just fine on my own,' she said, dutifully registering a protest vote.

He spun round to stare at her with incredulity.

'No, Maddie, you can't. The house is a mess. You haven't been eating. You've hired a team of builders who have obviously got the message that they can do as they please because you're too stressed out to stand your ground. You're too proud to ask for help. Whether you like it or not, you're going to pack two bags of summer clothes and we're going to fly out to my house first thing in the morning. Now, I can either pack those bags for you, or you can pack them yourself. When the bags are packed you're going to come back with me to my place, spend the night, and forget every single worry that's been dragging you down.'

'Since when did you become so bossy?'

Leo dealt her an amused, crooked smile.

'Sometimes being bossy is the only thing that works when you're dealing with a woman who digs her heels in so far that she refuses to ask for help even when she discovers she can't pull them out. Now, the bags…?'

Maddie gazed out of the window on the plane to the bank of clouds below. Everything had happened so fast that her head was still spinning. Put simply, Leo had taken over and, like a juggernaut, had bulldozed every single obstacle until she had left behind a trusted foreman who was going to supervise the work on the house with a rod of steel. And as far as the store was concerned he had moved in some of his own people.

'The store is yours,' he had told her before she'd been able to object, 'but you need the right resources to run it. I'll make sure you have them.'

Maddie had accepted without hesitation. Pride was one thing, but other people's livelihoods depended on her doing what she had set out to do with the store, and it had been proving more time-consuming and difficult than she had imagined. Pregnant, and with her head not entirely focused on the store, she had been distracted. And in the evenings she was very, very tired. Too tired to commit to the gruelling hours necessary at this stage in the process of taking the store out of the doldrums. And there was a limit to how much she could ask her trusted employees to do.

Leo would not take advantage. She knew that. She'd spent the past few weeks coming to terms with the fact that he was a man who was true to his word—a completely different species from Adam, with whom she had first so rashly compared him.

Leo was honourable to a fault. His proposal to her had been the ultimate act of selflessness, because he didn't love her, had never planned on having any sort of relationship with her after that one heady night of sex, and had never factored marriage to any woman into his agenda. He had his reasons, and she was guessing that he'd been hurt just as she had, but that aside she'd always known that he was not a guy in it for the long term. Yet, he'd bitten the bullet and proposed because he'd felt it was the right thing to do.

Not once over the past few weeks had he tried to bully her into marrying him either. He had obeyed all the *Do Not Trespass* signs she had posted without complaint. And that was pretty amazing, because she had thought that there was something fundamentally restless and impatient about him that would have had him crashing through any signs that didn't suit him.

She would not come back to find that the store had been converted into an electronics shop. Not that there was any chance of that anyway, because they would only be away for ten days.

She sneaked a sidelong glance at him. He was working, frowning slightly as he read through whatever was on his screen. He was perfectly still and yet he exuded the sort of energy that made her think of a resting tiger.

Ten days in his company…

How on earth was she going to cope?

Her heart picked up speed. Being in his company was a balancing act, and only now, with all the usual distractions removed, was she recognising that balancing act for what it was. A breathless mixture of excitement and apprehension, a forbidden longing that defied logic, and a need to get close to the fire even though it was dangerous.

It was okay when she was only seeing him now and again, only hearing that dark, velvety voice a couple of times a day. It was okay when there were other people around to dilute the force of his personality. But she quailed at the thought of being with him in an empty house.

'You never said…' She cleared her throat. 'Does anyone live in the…er…villa?'

Leo saved what he had been reading with the press of a key and angled his big body towards her in the first-class seat, which was generous but still somehow felt cramped to him.

'Anyone like who?' he drawled, amused by the delicate flush that had spread across her high cheekbones.

He'd expected her to fight him when it came to this trip because she seemed to want to fight him on everything, but she had conceded quickly and with a hint of relief.

Life was tough when you had no experience of the big, bad world of business—and when you'd made it your mission not to ask for help from the one person who could help you. Maddie was finding that out for herself and, whilst he was furious that she had allowed the situation to get out of hand before coming to him, he knew that he had finally found a way in to her.

He'd played the waiting game and he'd soon got fed up with it. It wasn't his style. Now that waiting game was over. He would show her just how good her life could be with him in it.

There was no way he was going to let her go down any road that saw him being pushed into second place in the parent stakes—arranging visits and watching from the sidelines while some other guy took the reins.

But any threat of a custody battle wouldn't do him any favours. Leo was very realistic about that. He worked long hours and, whilst he might have bottom-less funds when it came to providing financial security, it would be crazy to think that a live-in nanny would be any match for Maddie. No sane judge would rule in his favour. He wouldn't contemplate any such course of action. Because if he did, and subsequently lost, the price he would end up paying would be high.

Time had not been his friend. But he intended to make sure that it would be from now on, and being with her, a little voice said, wasn't exactly going to be a hardship. She had the oddest talent when it came to lifting his spirits, even though *accommodating* and *acquiescent* were two words that could never be used to describe her. and he'd always plumped for those two things when it came to the opposite sex.

'Staff?' Maddie ventured, wondering what sort of

staff manned a villa that was empty most of the year. 'You haven't really said much about it. How big is it? And why on earth do you have a villa on an island in the Caribbean if you hardly ever go there?'

'Investment,' Leo said succinctly. 'I tend to use it as a company retreat. Occasionally as a bonus holiday for high achievers. So, yes, there's staff. When it's empty they come in twice weekly, to air the place and make sure nothing's amiss, but it's used fairly frequently so they're kept busy much of the time. They're all on hefty retainers, so they're there whenever I need them.'

'Wow. Sometimes…'

'Sometimes?'

'Sometimes when you say stuff like that—like when you said that you would stay in Ireland and buy a house and it wouldn't be a problem because you could throw money at it—I realise just how *different* we are from one another.'

'Different doesn't necessarily mean incompatible.'

'Leo, before I went to work for Lacey I scrubbed floors. My mum worked all the hours God gave to make ends meet. She didn't get a penny from my grandfather…'

No surprise there, Leo thought. Old Tommaso, if his own grandfather could be believed, had forgotten how to spend money unless it was on drink or horses. He certainly wouldn't have been sending any to the daughter he'd excommunicated because of her lifestyle choices.

He'd made it quite clear—and indeed Leo had read the letter sent to his grandfather years ago, after his last purchase attempt of the store had hit a brick wall—that selling the store was as pie in the sky as welcoming back his wayward daughter.

'Too proud to ask, I'll bet…' Maddie said sadly.

'Really?'

'She could be stubborn.'

'The family resemblance is duly noted,' Leo remarked wryly.

Maddie blushed. 'I've never had a holiday, and when I came over here it was the first time I'd been on a plane.'

'We grew up in very different backgrounds,' Leo conceded, 'but we share some very similar traits. I've never known any woman as bloody stubborn as me, or as determined to set a course and stick to it.' He looked at her narrowly. 'Occasionally a person has to dig beneath the surface.'

'You're only saying that because I'm pregnant with your baby and you have to find *some* positives.'

'If that bastard ex of yours was around,' Leo said grimly, 'I'd flatten him.'

Maddie pinkened with pleasure at the possessiveness in Leo's voice. 'He did me a favour. He made me careful about trusting people.'

'He took away your confidence, and for that he deserves to be ripped apart limb by limb.'

'I'm just being realistic. Anyway… You haven't said… Will the house be staffed?'

'There will just be the two of us.' He shrugged, 'So there won't be any need to have the place swamped with staff. There will be a discreet service—a skeleton staff—and they, naturally, will not live in. No need for you to do anything at all on the domestic front, and I feel we're perfectly capable of taking care of our own breakfasts,'

'Of course,' Maddie said faintly. 'I've been doing that

all my life. I think I've got my technique well-honed when it comes to putting some cereal in a bowl or boiling an egg and making some toast.'

Leo's mouth twitched with amusement. 'I find it tiresome if there are people hovering when I want privacy…'

Maddie wondered what sort of privacy Leo had in mind, and had to soothe herself with the timely reminder that he was no longer interested in her as a sexual being. She was carrying his child and had now entered a different category. He'd gone from wanting her to wanting to make sure she was okay—which was a completely different thing.

But she wanted him to care because of *her* and not just because of the fact that she was carrying his baby. She wanted to crawl into his arms and have him hold her because he wanted to—not because he was concerned about her stress levels because of the baby…

She pushed the thought away.

'You won't have to think about anything while you're out there, Maddie,' he continued.

'That's a big promise, Leo.' She laughed, surprised at how relaxed she felt in his company—but then, when she'd first met him she'd felt relaxed as well.

For a moment he wasn't Leo the billionaire, who'd wanted her store and was now stuck with her because of the pregnancy, but the Leo who had charmed her with his wit and humour and mind-blowing sex appeal.

'I've never been in a situation where I haven't had to think about *something*, so I'm not sure how I would cope with that.'

She blushed when he fixed his amazing eyes on her with thoughtful, speculative intensity.

'You haven't had an easy life,' he conceded, 'but now you're pregnant, and your days of having to stress and worry are over.'

'I'm not a piece of china.' But the protest was half-hearted.

'You are to me.'

Maddie blushed a little more, rattled because there was something intimate about what he was saying—even though she knew that he was just reiterating what he'd said from the beginning, which was that she was his responsibility now that she was pregnant, whether she liked it or not.

She cleared her throat but couldn't quite meet his gaze. 'I shouldn't complain anyway. I have a lot to be thankful for, thanks to my grandfather's legacy. I have the store, and a roof over my head, and sufficient money to have secured the bank loan. I just wish,' she confessed, 'that I could have met him.'

'Tommaso?' Leo looked at her, startled. 'Why?'

'What do you mean *why*?' Maddie asked. 'I never knew my dad. My mum ran away from her family—precious little of it as there was—and severed all ties. There was always just me and my mum. And, yes, she used to say that we were two against the world, but I would really have liked it to have been *lots* of us against the world. Two is such a lonely number… I knew I was never going to meet my father, and I never wanted to, but I would have loved to have met my grandfather—especially as I think that he probably wanted to meet me, to have Mum relent…'

'What gives you *that* idea?'

'He left everything to me,' Maddie said flatly. 'Why else would he have done that?'

'Because it's the Italian way,' Leo said drily.

'You're so cynical, Leo.'

'He was never going to leave his dwindling fortune to the local cat sanctuary.'

She looked away, her chin at a defiant angle, heated colour still tingeing her cheeks.

Leo could see that Maddie wanted to believe the best of Tommaso—was desperate to forge a link with the grandfather she'd never known—and taking care of the store was part of that. She obviously had no idea what the wily fox had really been like, and on the spot Leo decided that that was something he would never reveal. Let her keep her dreams.

Besides, instigating show-downs and arguments wasn't part of his agenda.

He relaxed and said soothingly, 'To the best of my knowledge, he was no animal lover. And perhaps you're right—perhaps it was his way of reaching out to you from beyond the grave…'

'You think so?'

The urge to burst out laughing died on his lips as he took in the earnestness of her expression, the *hope*. Not for the first time, he cursed the old bastard who had stubbornly refused to make amends with his only child—and with the grandchild he had never seen.

'I'm sure that's exactly how it was,' he said gravely.

Leo had always wanted the store—had promised his grandfather he'd get it—but he knew that he wasn't going to stamp out Maddie's curiously romanticised dreams to get his way, and knew that his grandfather would understand. Frankly, the prospect of a great-grandchild would be a heck of a lot more exciting to the old man.

'Mum never talked about any of it. She was way too proud. I sometimes wonder whether I should have pressed her more for answers.'

'Why didn't you?'

'I knew it would upset her.'

'Understandable,' Leo said in a low, roughened undertone. 'And of course it's only when we're older that we have the confidence to tackle our parents on an adult footing. Respect often gets in the way of interrogation, and I guess by the time you came of age you were wrapped up in having to deal with much bigger issues because your mother was ill.'

Maddie looked astounded at his understanding of just where she was coming from.

'Don't beat yourself up over that,' he said, more briskly. 'I find it never pays to dwell on the past. In less than four hours you're going to be at my villa, without a care in the world. I have everything at the store under control, and my team will be reporting daily on work to your house.'

Returning to his laptop—because there was such a thing as too much touchy-feely, *let's get the tissues out and have a good old cry* bonding—he glanced at her out of the corner of his eye and saw, with great satisfaction, that when she lay back and closed her eyes all traces of anxiety had been wiped clean from her face.

CHAPTER EIGHT

MADDIE HAD NO real idea what to expect at the end of the nine-hour trip—mostly by plane, but for the final leg on the small speedboat which had been waiting for them at the marina. But any awkwardness at being so far removed from her comfort zone with Leo was dispelled in her speechless wonderment at the stunning island on which they finally found themselves.

Evening was fast approaching, and as they were taken from one marina on the main island to be deposited at another marina on its much smaller sister, she could just about appreciate the scenery as it was gradually absorbed into darkness. Burnt orange skies turned to violet, then finally to star-pricked black, and she saw lush vegetation, soft, rounded hills, a main road that was just big enough for two cars to pass side by side, and banks upon banks of gently swaying coconut trees, tall and spindly and graceful.

'It's stunning,' she breathed, her head swinging from left to right as the car which had been waiting for them, and which Leo was now handling like an expert, bounced along the uneven road.

There was virtually no traffic at all. But lights from occupied houses could be glimpsed as they went along.

This was the enclave of the super-rich—an island on which they could relax without fear of paparazzi or nosy neighbours with binoculars.

Somewhere close to the marina they had left behind was a small but functioning town, where the essentials could be purchased and where several high-end restaurants catered for the island's wealthy visitors, and for anyone else who wanted to travel by boat from the main island and enjoy the top-rated cuisine.

Leo explained all this as they drove towards his villa. His voice was low and soothing, and the melodious background noise of the sea was achieving the impossible and making her forget all about the stress she had left behind in Ireland.

Leo had promised her complete rest and relaxation and he was already delivering on that promise big-time. She hadn't felt this rested in a long, long time.

Sneaking a sideways glance at his strong profile as he concentrated on driving, she felt her body respond in the way she had tried so hard to train it not to do. Her breathing slowed and her eyelids fluttered and she was assailed by total recall of how those strong hands had felt roaming all over her body.

She pushed those thoughts away to the back of her mind because they were inappropriate. She and Leo had to grope their way to a new and different footing, and getting turned on by him had no place in that scenario.

They would share a child and have a cordial but detached relationship. There could be nothing else for them. Because she could never and *would* never marry anyone who had to be dragged up the aisle like a prisoner in handcuffs. She deserved better—no matter what he said about two parents being better than one. She *knew* that two parents were better than one! But only if those parents had married for the right reasons.

What if *her* parents had decided to stick together because of *her*? Would her childhood have been picture-perfect with a disillusioned and bitter mother and a father manacled against his will? He would only have wanted marriage for the fortune he'd anticipated getting out of her mother, and would have suddenly found himself anchored down because of a child on the way.

Needless to say that was a fairly impossible scenario to imagine, because her father hadn't had an ounce of responsibility running through his veins, but still...

And yet for all that sensible reasoning, with the balmy night air outside and the foreign sight of a velvety black sky dotted with stars, Maddie *was* turned on—as though a dimmer switch had been buzzing in the background and had suddenly been turned to full beam.

She shifted, and was alarmed at the suffocating sense of *want*.

It was almost a relief when the car rounded a bend and there was the villa, lit up on the outside. It was ranch-style, with a massive outer veranda that seemed to circle the whole impressive building like a necklace. They drove into the courtyard, with Leo making innocuous conversation about the island and what she might expect by way of entertainment.

Which was very little from the sounds of it.

'I hate clubs anyway,' Maddie said distractedly as she stared at the villa and tried to get her head around how much her life had changed in the space of a few months.

She rested her hand on her stomach and for a few seconds wished that the perfect life she'd always dreamed of had materialised. With a baby on the way and financial security, and finally feeling well and truly over her stupid, ill-advised ex, things should have been so good—but what promised so much on the outside was riddled with rot on the inside, and she couldn't get away from that.

Leo didn't care about her. He was doing all this because of the baby. If it weren't for the new life she was carrying he would have waged a no-holds-barred attack on her in order to get the store, and the single night they had shared would have been a distant memory.

He didn't care about her.

But she cared about him.

She shivered and tried to unravel that thought so that she could pick it apart and make a nonsense of it. But it had formed and it refused to budge.

She cared about him.

She might have thrown caution to the wind and slept with him for all the right reasons, but she had remained connected to him after sex, even though she'd barely been aware of it.

And then finding out she was pregnant... That had opened a door and allowed all sorts of things to enter—all sorts of emotions that she hadn't been able to staunch. She'd seen beyond the billionaire. And once that had happened she'd been seduced by all the complex sides of him that showed him to be honourable, decent, fair...

She'd fallen for those traits.

She'd fallen for the guy who had stepped up to the plate when it had mattered and had backed off when she had told him to.

Maddie had to remind herself strenuously of all the reasons she had told him to back off, because in a moment of weakness, as he drew to a stop and then turned to look at her, his beautiful face all shadows and angles, she wondered what she had done.

He'd proposed marriage and she'd turned him down flat. Why? Had he been right? Had she been selfish?

She could do a lot worse than marry someone who was *not* the sort of ruthless money-making machine she had written him off as being. And who knew? He could come to love her. Couldn't he?

Maddie hated having those thoughts, because she knew how dangerous they were.

'Hello?' Leo interrupted drily. 'I've lost you. Please don't tell me that you've suddenly decided to get cold feet because you're going to be sharing a villa with me.'

'Huh?' Maddie blinked.

Leo contained his impatience. 'Separate quarters,' he told her abruptly, swinging out of the car and feeling the blast of late-evening humidity, hearing the orchestra of insects which was so much part and parcel of this part of the world.

Never had he had to curtail his energy and his driving need to act as much as over the past few hours. It was frustrating. He was the father of her child and prepared to do the decent thing. He was ready to sacrifice his freedom for the greater good. He couldn't understand why it was so damned hard for her to see that and accept it.

He prided himself on being a pretty unemotional guy, but now he was having to deal with irrational mood swings. One minute he was optimistic, determined to work his way into any cracks he could see, to find a foothold and frankly exploit it. The next minute he could smell her retreat and was at a loss as to whether to push forward or stand still. There was a helplessness to this situation that he found maddening, and it took all he had to tame his urge to *do something*.

His work was suffering. For the first time in his life he wasn't able to focus with the level of intensity he was so accustomed to. He was, for once, impotent. Unable to stamp his authority and get what he wanted, what he *knew* was right. And he *thought* about her. Without warning he would think about the sound of her laughter, or the way she sometimes looked at him out of the corner of her eye, or the things she said that could make him laugh out loud because her sense of humour so often mirrored his.

It was doing his head in.

'Separate quarters?' Maddie parroted.

'You needn't worry that your privacy is going to be invaded in any way,' Leo gritted, not looking at her but heaving the suitcases out of the car and preceding her into the villa. 'Although I should warn you in advance that there's no one here at the moment. We're both adults, and I didn't think it was necessary to have members of staff hovering here past their bedtime because we need chaperones.'

Maddie flushed, clearly apprehensive that he might not be able to restrain himself around her. Where would she have got that idea? Considering he'd backed right off and hadn't shown the slightest interest in her since she'd turned him down.

'Absolutely!' She smiled brightly and changed the subject. 'The villa is gorgeous, Leo. I'm surprised you don't want to retire here permanently!'

'Sun, sea and stars has never been my thing for longer than five minutes.'

Leo grinned that sexy grin that made her quiver inside.

'You're more wine, women and song?' Maddie quipped, following him into the villa and doing a complete turn as she absorbed her surroundings.

Cool shades of cream complemented wood and the bold silkscreen paintings on the walls. White shutters would keep the glare of the sun out. And as she wandered, agog, towards an expanse of glass towards the back of the villa, she glimpsed manicured lawns, lit up just as the front was.

When she turned around it was to find Leo looking at her—although he looked away as soon as their eyes met.

'Hungry?' he asked.

'A bit.'

'Kitchen's through here. Food will have been prepared and there will be no shortage of anything.'

'This is the most amazing house I've ever been in,' Maddie breathed, frankly awestruck and working hard to remember every socialist tendency that should be fighting to play down the shameless splendour of the villa.

Leo paused to look at her again, head tilted to one side. 'Funny, but I no longer notice my surroundings,' he mused truthfully.

'That's because you've always had far too much money,' she said sternly, and he burst out laughing, his navy eyes appreciative.

'I never thought I'd ever hear those words leave any woman's mouth.'

'Then you've been mixing with the wrong type of woman.'

She wasn't looking at him as she said this. She was

shamelessly peering out through the glass doors, squinting into the darkness, intrigued by the glimpse of an
illuminated infinity pool.

'What sort of women do you think I *should* have
been mixing with?'

Maddie started, because he had come up behind her
and she could see his reflection in the glass—a towering, impossibly forceful presence that gave her goose-
bumps. The urge to sink back against that hard body
was so overpowering that she inhaled deeply and stared
blindly, trying hard to block him from her line of vision.

'Well?'

Leo stepped closer towards her. He had managed to
angle the conversation into a place that felt highly personal, and suddenly he seemed determined to explore
all those places she was trying to keep hidden from
him—places where desire and lust were locked away.

'I—I don't know,' she stammered.

When she turned round it was to discover that he was
even closer to her than she'd thought. But if she stepped
back she'd bump into the glass. She was trapped with
only inches between them.

Maddie could feel the heat emanating from his body
in waves, and like a dose of incense it went to her head
and made her feel giddy. She licked her lips and tried
to think straight.

'Tut-tut,' Leo chided softly. 'You can't just make
sweeping statements and then refuse to back them up.
Do you think I should have been going out with earnest
young women who like nothing better than to spend an
evening discussing books?'

Maddie shifted and blushed. She tried to imagine
Leo with a woman fitting that description and hon-

estly couldn't think of *any* woman who wouldn't want to rip his clothes off within five seconds of occupying the same sofa as him.

'Well, they would have been better than women who like you for your money.'

'What makes you think that earnest young women who like discussing books wouldn't want me for my money? Wouldn't be impressed by all of this?' He spread his arms in an all-encompassing gesture, but his fabulous eyes remained firmly fixed to Maddie's face. 'After all, *you* are.'

Maddie glared at him and Leo laughed.

'But I do know that you weren't attracted to me because of my bank balance,' he murmured with satisfaction. 'Were you?'

Maddie muttered something inaudible. He was pinning her into a corner, standing just a fraction too close to her and looking at her just a little too intently and with slightly too much sexy humour for her to be comfortable.

Sex was off the menu!

But then she mentally kicked herself for even thinking that that would be going through his head. Leo was good at making her think all sorts of forbidden thoughts just by doing what he was doing now—getting just a little too much under her skin. He probably didn't even realise what he was doing!

Restless in her own skin, Maddie stared down for a few seconds and fidgeted.

'I really like that about you…'

Leo placed one finger under her chin in a barely there touch and Maddie immediately looked up, bright green eyes meeting deepest blue.

Suddenly she had somehow managed to turn into a swooning Victorian maiden—the same swooning maiden who had been bowled over by him, enough to leap into bed with him before he'd even finished asking. And as far as impulse decisions went, how clever had *that* one been? Considering she was standing here now, pregnant with his baby?

And yet...

When Maddie went through those 'sliding doors' and thought about the other road she might have gone down, she knew that she preferred this one.

What if he hadn't been after her store? What if he had genuinely been who he'd said he was? Or *implied* he was? A sexy guy just passing through—another rolling stone looking for adventure?

One night of passion and that would have been it. She would never have lain eyes on him again. She couldn't get her head around the enormity of that, because he had managed to become such a huge part of her life—always there in her thoughts in one way or another.

With the less attractive option—and the reason why she had to stand firm against the pulsing tide of craving that threatened to breach her defences the second she took her eye off the ball—came the realisation that under normal circumstances, and without a baby on the way, she *would* have met him again.

They would have had their one night and then she would have met the real Leo—the billionaire who wanted what she had and would stop at nothing to get his hands on it. He wouldn't have been toting her off to this fabulous villa in a tropical paradise. He would have been sitting, steely eyed, on the opposite side of a boardroom table while his team of lawyers tried to prise the store away from her. He wouldn't have given a damn about the sentiment wrapped up in her need to do something with her legacy. She would have been disposable.

Unfortunately nothing could stop the ache inside her when their eyes locked. It was as if he had somehow programmed her brain to ignore common sense. She could give herself a thousand bracing lectures about why she couldn't afford to let her body do the talking, but the second he did what he was doing now—looking at her *like that*—she was all lust and craving and weak-kneed desire.

'You bucked the trend,' Leo continued in the same musing low voice, as rich and as silky as the finest chocolate. 'You thought I had nothing and you weren't bothered. In fact what bothered you was thinking that you might have more than me...'

'I'm suspicious of rich guys after Adam,' Maddie breathed. 'And besides, I was raised not to place too much importance on money. I guess, when I look back, that was my mother's response to being disinherited. She'd given up everything for love. She couldn't start telling me that the only thing that mattered was money. But she must have found it so hard—especially in the beginning, when she could still remember what it was like to have everything she wanted at the snap of a finger.'

'Like I said...you bucked the trend...'

Maddie was mesmerised by his eyes, weakly unable to tear her gaze away. She blinked and gathered herself against the riptide pulling her under. 'Poor Leo. What a daily strain it must be, having to beat back women who want nothing more than to do whatever you want and fall into bed with you.'

Leo laughed and stepped back—which at least meant that she could breathe without fear that her airways would start closing up.

'Fortunately,' he drawled, 'I'm made of stern stuff, and I've found that I can handle that thorny dilemma reasonably well. Now, shall I show you to your quarters? You can shower and then join me for something to eat. It's late, but you need to fatten up.'

Wrenched out of her heated torpor, Maddie took a few seconds to establish that Leo was back to his usual self—casual and courteous and practically whistling a merry tune as he spun round and began sauntering off into the bowels of the sprawling villa.

She tripped along, soon catching up with him. She'd packed only one suitcase, which he'd retrieved from the airy hallway. When she reached for her carry-on he tut-tutted in a fashion that made her teeth snap together in frustration and took it from her.

'I'm not completely helpless, Leo,' she said, her mouth downturned and resentful because she knew that, however appropriate it was, this was not how she wished to be treated by him.

'In my eyes you are,' he purred, ignoring her tight-lipped expression and favouring her with a smile that was an annoying combination of ruefulness and pure charm. 'I hope this will do...'

He pushed open a door that led to the most wonderful bedroom Maddie had ever seen. The white wooden shutters were closed, but she knew that when they were open the light would flood in, because they covered the expanse of one entire wall. The king-sized bed was draped in the finest of mosquito nets, and the room was cooled by air-conditioning that was virtually silent. The décor, like in the rest of the villa, was pale. Cream walls, light bamboo furniture and an oversized squashy pale lemon sofa next to a door that led directly out onto the veranda that circled the house.

Leo was striding to another door, which he pushed open in the manner of an estate agent keen to show a prospective buyer all the home comforts.

'En-suite bathroom,' he said, and Maddie walked towards him and peered into a room the size of the apartment she had shared with her mother in Sydney.

Through an archway leading from the bedroom was a spacious sitting area, complete with a giant flat screen television and all the accoutrements of an office—which was the only indicator that the villa was used for work purposes much of the time.

He returned to the bedroom and stood to one side of the huge bed. 'Think you'll be comfortable?'

Maddie stared at him, mouth dry, and tried to get her wayward thoughts back in order—because seeing him there next to the bed was resurrecting all sorts of unfortunate memories.

She half closed her eyes and pictured his lean, muscular body splayed across the puffy white duvet, bronzed and hard and *naked*.

'It's perfect,' she croaked, jerkily heading to her suitcase and flipping it open so that he would get the message that it was time for him to leave.

Which he did.

'If you need anything…' Leo pointed to a bell which she hadn't noticed on the table next to the bed '…summon me…'

'Really?' Maddie almost smiled at his use of the expression. Without thinking, she added, half to herself,

'And what would you do?' Then she realised what she'd said and reddened.

'*You're* here to do nothing,' Leo told her, straight-faced, 'so basically I'll do whatever you want.'

The quiet charge of electricity thrummed between them.

'Oh? You'd cook and clean for me?' Maddie quipped, perversely tempted to keep him in the bedroom now that he was clearly itching to leave. 'Somehow I can't picture you doing *any* of that stuff, Leo.'

'Cleaning might be a problem,' he conceded with amusement. 'But I could definitely rise to the challenge of cooking—although there will be no need for that, bearing in mind I have round-the-clock staff who are paid to take care of those duties.'

For the first time in living memory he didn't flinch at the vision of domesticity that presented itself to him. He had a strangely satisfying vision of her resting on the sofa in his living room, heavy with his child, while he brought her home-cooked food.

He'd never cooked anything that hadn't come with printed instructions on the packet in which it was wrapped, but he was sure he could rustle up something and he rather enjoyed playing with that thought. Maybe in due course he would invest in a recipe book. Who knew? His life was changing, and it was going to change even more dramatically after the baby was born. Could he say with any certainty that he *wouldn't* be spending evenings in, wearing an apron and brandishing a spatula in front of the stove?

He grinned. The faster you accepted the inevitable, the better off you were. *Fact.*

He was pro-active, creative, solution-orientated, and

he seldom wasted energy pushing boulders up hills when they were very likely to come rolling right back down.

If you worked with what you'd got, however troublesome, you usually ended up coming out the victor. And, since Leo intended to come out the victor in this scenario, he was proud of the unusual tramline his thoughts were travelling along.

'Of course,' Maddie said politely.

'Although,' he mused, 'I might relieve them of some of their culinary duties.'

He wondered where the pots and pans were kept. It was an area of the kitchen he'd never felt the need to explore.

'Why would you do that?'

'Necessity,' Leo said succinctly. He lowered his eyes and looked at her lazily, each syllable leaving his mouth replete with intent. 'You will find that I'm a man who doesn't take shortcuts when it comes to the things that matter to me. My child will top that list. Having someone else prepare food will naturally work occasionally, but I'll do much of that myself.'

'You will?'

'What sort of father do you think I will be?'

'I—I haven't really given it much thought,' Maddie stammered, caught on the back foot at this unexpected tangent.

'I'm sure you have,' Leo responded wryly. 'Just as I'm sure that I don't emerge in those thoughts with flying colours. You think I would be an unsuitable rich husband who fails to live up to the storybook image in your head, and a likewise unsuitable rich father who thinks that money can take the place of time.'

'I've never thought anything of the sort!'

'Of course you did. At the risk of disillusioning you, I intend to be a hands-on father. My work life will be tailored to accommodate my child. I didn't envisage myself in the role of a father until it was sprung on me, but now that I am I will be giving it everything I have.'

He patiently waited for her to pounce. He almost felt that he knew her better than she knew herself.

Maddie shuffled as she sifted through what he was saying. Okay, so maybe she *had* been guilty of type-casting him as the wealthy but absent parent—but was that her fault? Workaholics were never interested in the small stuff, were they? Since when could she have expected the most eligible bachelor on the planet to willingly immerse himself in nappy-changing duties?

Was he just saying that to make a good impression? No, why should he?

'So cooking practice might be just the thing.' Leo paused and looked at her after a moment's silence. 'And of course,' he continued, 'it would carry on, I imagine, even after I have found someone…'

'Found someone?' Maddie looked at him, disorientated. 'What are you talking about?'

'Well,' Leo said crisply, all business now, wrapping up their little *tête-à-tête* just at the point when she was hanging on to his every word, her heart beating like a crazy, caged bird inside her chest, 'you don't think that while you're roaming the streets in search of Prince Charming I'm going to be sitting in my apartment keeping the home fires burning as I pine for the marriage that never was, do you?'

Leo let the silence settle between them like a piece of lead dropping into still water, only to send concentric ripples across the surface, turning the stillness into a frenzy of motion.

He was by the bedroom door now, and he lounged against the doorframe, his lean, rangy body relaxed and at ease.

'Of course not!' Maddie was aware of her voice sounding a little less stable than usual and she cleared her throat.

'Good!' he said brightly. 'Because I won't be.'

'Although I really don't think it's acceptable for any child to be exposed to a constant carousel of women coming and going,' she protested stoutly, and Leo raised his eyebrows with an expression she understood completely. She was quick to clarify. 'I have no intention of entertaining a series of men in front of any child of mine!'

'And you have my word that I will likewise be extremely discreet in all *my* relationships.'

He watched as she fidgeted and stared at him. For a few seconds he was distracted by the lushness of her parted mouth and the soft little breaths coming from her. It surprised him how many of her mannerisms he had absorbed over time—right down to the way she had just tossed her hair back in a gesture that was proud, feisty and unconsciously sexy.

He had no intention of stressing her out. He had brought her here so that she could *de*-stress. But neither was he going to spend this valuable one-on-one time tiptoeing around her and waiting patiently for her to come to her senses.

When they returned to London and Benito was back from his cruise, he would condescend to meet the mother of his much longed-for grandchild, and Leo intended the picture to be complete, with wedding bells chiming in the not too distant future if not immediately imminent. He knew that Benito Conti would be bitterly disappointed to be presented with a complicated scenario of joint custody and visiting rights.

'The only woman our child will meet will be the woman who will become his or her stepmother.'

A dull pain spread through Maddie, making her limbs heavy. She suddenly wanted to be sick, because this very likely possibility was one she had not considered in much detail. She'd been far too wrapped up in standing her ground and refusing to compromise on her principles.

'I know you'll agree with me that our child would benefit from that.'

'So you wouldn't object if *I* found someone else?'

'What could I do?'

Leo gritted his teeth and controlled the insane thought that he would be tempted to pummel whoever she happened to find, which had to be double standards at their very worst.

'As you pointed out, isn't that the way of the world these days? Split families and children being ferried from one set of parents to the other? Half-brothers and stepsisters and stepfathers and Christmas celebrated ten times a year so that everyone can get a look-in?'

Maddie didn't reply, because she was busy wondering what this wife-to-be of his would look like. It was galling, but true, that whilst as a single mother her ranking on the eligibility scale would plummet, he, as a single father, would discover that his had hit the stratosphere.

There was nothing a woman loved more than a guy

with a baby. It brought out every maternal instinct in them. Throw *rich beyond belief* and *sinfully sexy* into the mix and Leo would be lucky if he could get two steps out of his penthouse apartment before finding a queue of eager candidates waiting to interview for the job of perfect stepmother to his child. *Her* child!

'But enough of this,' he concluded. 'Towels should be in the bathroom, and there are more beauty products in the cupboard than on the beauty counter at the store. I gave very precise instructions as to the stocking of essentials while we were here.'

'Okay…' Maddie said, in a daze.

'No routine out here. I will continue working for much of the day, but I'm sure I can find time to show you around the island. Primarily, though, you're to do as you please. Come and go as you want. You may have spotted the swimming pool? You'll find it quite stunning. It overlooks the ocean. If you need anything at all, there's the bell…'

He grinned and gave her a little half-salute, but she was too distracted to respond in kind. Instead she nodded, and found that she actually needed to force herself to breathe when the bedroom door had closed quietly behind him.

CHAPTER NINE

'I'VE MADE A SCHEDULE,' Leo said, brandishing a printed sheet of paper as Maddie walked into the kitchen the following morning at a little after nine.

'You should have woken me up,' she said, sniffing and clearly detecting the smell of bacon. 'I never get up this late.'

'It's important that you get your rest.' He ushered her to a chair and sat her down. 'Sleep well?'

'Have you…*cooked*?'

'"Cooked" is a big word. I prefer to say *dabbled*. I thought I'd give the staff some time off while we're here. After all, in my role of *father* I'm going to have to function without a team of people picking up the pieces behind me all the time.'

Leo had had time to think. She disliked the notion of marriage as a business transaction. She wanted romance. She wanted to be swept off her feet by the perfect guy. He wasn't the perfect guy for her, and he wasn't going to pretend that he was. He wasn't going to wax lyrical about love. But he *was* going to show her what he was made of when it came to fulfilling his responsibilities.

As a bonus, he would also be showing her what another woman might find appealing. Goodbye Leo the womaniser and hello Leo the dutiful dad with apron and spatula. And, of course, the baby…

All's fair in love and war, he thought and finding solutions to problems was his forte, whatever the problem might be.

This was his solution and he was going to bring everything to the table.

'So what did you…er…*dabble* in?' Maddie asked.

'Bacon. Eggs. Bread.' He brought two plates to the table and continued doing whatever he was doing with his back to her, a tea towel slung over one shoulder.

He looked drop-dead gorgeous, and Maddie had to stare. He was wearing low-slung khaki shorts and a faded tee shirt and he was barefoot. With his back to her, she could appreciate the long lines of his lean body, the strength of his muscular legs, the width of his broad shoulders.

It didn't seem fair that a man in old clothes with a tea towel over his shoulder should look so mouthwatering.

Any woman looking at him right now wouldn't be able to resist.

Stick a baby in a high chair next to him and he'd have to beat them away with sticks.

She felt queasy thinking about it.

'Have you ever done anything this…ambitious… before?'

Leo produced a big white plate on which some charred bacon sat, spread across four fried eggs.

'Timing may have been an issue,' Leo declared, fetching a heaping mound of toast, 'but practice will make perfect. Eat up. You need to get nutrients into you after the fiasco with your kitchen. By the way, I got an email this morning. Things are already moving on that front.'

'Really?' Maddie helped herself to a slice of toast and then to one of the less dangerously overcooked rashers of bacon. 'But it's only been a matter of a day...'

'I said I'd sort it, and it'll be sorted in record time. I snap my fingers and people jump. Now, about this schedule.'

'Schedule?'

'I don't want you feeling bored while you're here.'

'Leo, I don't think it would be possible to feel bored here. There's the pool and the wonderful gardens to explore, and I'm very happy to wander into town and have a look around. I don't want you to think that you have to put yourself out for me.'

Leo paused, fork raised to his mouth, and looked at her. 'Wander into town?' In that little flowered sundress that made her look as pure as the driven snow and as sexy as the hottest siren? Over his dead body. No one would guess that she was pregnant. She'd be knee-deep in lecherous men within seconds.

'A tour of the island.' He swept aside her contribution and carried on eating. 'I have a boat docked in one of the sheltered bays. Nothing fancy.'

'You keep a boat here? Whatever for, when you hardly use the villa?'

'Guests at the villa are welcome to use it. It gets used. How are you on the swimming front?'

'I'm not exactly a fish...'

'I thought Australia was all about the outdoor life...?'

'Swimming lessons are pricey. I'm a self-taught swimmer. I get by, but I wouldn't put money on my chances of surviving in a riptide.'

'Then it's just as well,' Leo said smugly, 'that I'll be there every step of the way to keep an eye on you. Fortunately I'm a first-class swimmer.'

Maddie rolled her eyes. He was determined to treat her like an invalid. She should protest, but there was a warm, cosy feeling inside her created by the attention and she was rather enjoying it.

She'd never had attention—not really. Her mother had loved her, but she had been so busy working to make ends meet that there hadn't been time for lots of bonding sessions, and for the last few years of her life *she* had been the one requiring attention.

Then Maddie had gone into the business of caring for Lacey. And when Adam had come along, she had basked in the glow of thinking that she was loved. But, looking back, she could see that Adam had dressed her like a doll to be showcased, and had never shown that he loved her for who she was when she wasn't draped in the latest fashions and expensive jewellery. She could see now that he had been so conscious of the disparity in their status that cossetting her had never even occurred to him. She'd been arm candy. Nothing more.

There had been no other relatives in her life to lean on—no siblings, no doting grandparents, no aunts or uncles or cousins.

So what was the harm in accepting a little pampering from Leo?

'So, if you get your swimsuit…' He stood up briskly. 'I'll meet you in the hall in say…half an hour?'

'We should tidy the kitchen.'

'Leave all that.' Leo removed the plate from her hand. 'I'll deal with it later, once we're back from our day's activities.'

'We're going for *the day*?'

'Unless you have an unavoidable appointment?'

'No, but…'

Don't do this, don't be so nice that I start regretting my decision.

'What about work?'

'I can't remember the last time I had a holiday. A few days off isn't going to kill me. And, anyway, I'm keeping on top of things via email.'

Maddie was amused and a little relieved to find out that there would be no burnt offerings for lunch, because forty minutes later they were swinging by one of the few restaurants in the town, where he collected a picnic hamper and a cooler bag of drinks.

It was hot, the sun beating down from a cloudless turquoise sky, and the island was so small that it was possible to see the distant strip of sea from either side of the car as it bumped along away from the town.

Fringes of coconut trees lined the small ribbon of road, stretching into the distance—banks of them like upright soldiers on parade.

Every so often she would see a flash of deep blue sea, and then, after twenty minutes of driving, they were ploughing down a rocky incline and pulling into a cove.

It was a private beach, small but perfectly formed. Backed into the shrubbery among the coconut trees was a small cabin, and moored to one side was the boat he had told her about.

'How many properties like these do you own?' she asked as he swung round to help her out of the Jeep.

'A handful. All investment places. Some used slightly more than others.'

'Don't you get tired of London? Want to escape to some place like this?'

'I've never been good at escaping,' Leo confessed. He looked at her and then brushed some of her hair away from her face.

'If you were born into money...'

She bent down to pull off her sandals and Leo drew in a sharp breath, causing her to look up, catch his eyes on her cleavage and the black swimsuit holding in her pouting breasts, which were bigger and fuller now with her new pregnant figure. She looked away and quickly straightened, hopping a little because the sand was hot.

'Then surely you must have had loads of opportunity to do whatever you wanted...'

'I must have been born with an over-developed responsibility gene. That sand's hot.' He swept her off her feet and carried her to the cabin. 'Make sure you apply lots of sunblock. I'm going to fetch the hamper and we can relax for a while before we take the boat out.'

Maddie looked at him for a while, silent and speculative. He *did* that. He only told her what he wanted her to know. He never spoke about anything personal and she wished she could get into his head and prise out his secrets. He knew all hers!

'Okay.'

She shrugged. She was going to enjoy the day and enjoy being away from the chaos of the house and the weight of running the store.

The cabin was small but exquisite, as lovely as anything money could buy. She opened the few doors and peered into two bedrooms and two bathrooms, a bedroom and another bathroom on either side of a wooden-floored sitting area and an open-plan kitchen. Lots of squashy sofas and low tables.

She replaced her dress with a sarong and rubbed sun-block all over. She was used to the sun, having lived in Australia, and knew that taking chances was never a good idea, even though she tanned easily.

She looked in the full-length mirror and saw a girl who looked radiant. Her skin had deepened over the summer to the colour of a latte—her Italian ancestry shining through. Her hair was almost down to her waist. When she turned to the side she could see the small but definite bump of her tummy.

The biggest change to her appearance, though, was that the misery of the past few years and the horror of what had happened to her before she'd left Australia were no longer etched on her face.

She looked...*happy*. She was pregnant after a one-night stand, the house she had inherited had been all but dismantled the last time she'd set eyes on it, and the responsibility of running the store was a weight that couldn't be underestimated because other people's live-lihoods were at stake, and yet she was *happy*.

Happy to be right here, right now, with a man who wasn't in love with her and never would be. Just happy to be around him.

It was a frightening thought, and it made her heart beat fast—because there could only be one reason why she felt so content, despite the many things that should be concerning her.

Leo didn't love her, but that didn't mean *she* hadn't fallen for *him*—because she had. He'd got under her skin, and now that he had lodged there she couldn't prise him away.

Ever since she'd become pregnant he'd been a rock, and never more so than now. He was determined to prove just how solid he could be and it was a seductive tactic—because it was making her rethink the decision she had made.

Still pensive, she went out to find that he had set up camp under a canopy of coconut trees. She took a few seconds to absorb the setting. Powdery white sand sloping down to crystal-clear water as blue as the sky above it...rocks and coconut trees embracing the cove...the brightly painted boat now bobbing in the water to one side...and Leo, hunky and sexy and willing to cook her breakfast because he felt she needed looking after.

Had she been seeing everything from a skewed perspective? Instead of bemoaning the fact that he was protective because of the baby she was carrying and not because of *her*, should she instead just be seeing his drive to be protective as something to be lauded? As an indication of his strength of character and his fundamental decency?

Her formative experience with men had come in the form of her father, who had jumped ship and bailed on wedlock the second he'd discovered that her mother came without the dowry he'd banked on. And then Adam, who had treated her like a mannequin and then dumped her when she'd been accused of theft because he'd thought that someone who didn't come from his class couldn't possibly have principles.

And yet, despite her experiences, she realised she'd put a lot of faith in love. Heck, she'd dug her heels in and turned down Leo's marriage proposal because he didn't love her.

But what she'd failed to appreciate was that there

were all sorts of counter-arguments for the deal he'd proposed that made a lot of sense. Including the fact that not marrying him meant she'd have to face the idea of him not being in her life after the baby was born.

Leo glanced across and saw her standing there, looking at him pensively. She quickly looked away, out towards the water, but she wasn't fast enough to miss the appreciative glance he cast over her rounded stomach, which he was seeing for the first time. She suddenly realised how little the wisp of floaty fabric tied around her waist did to cover her.

'Have you remembered the sunblock?' he asked, with a hint of some deeper thought in his voice.

Maddie remembered that her feeling resentful because his concern was solely directed with the baby in mind should not be on the cards, and so she smiled and nodded.

'It's practically a criminal offence to go out without sunblock in Australia. You're really well prepared for a day at the beach, Leo.' She eyed the picture-perfect oversized towel, the hamper, the fluffy beach towels rolled into sausage shapes.

'I'm going to put the food inside,' he responded. 'Then what about a bit of sailing?'

'Are you sure…'

'That I'm a master sailor? Yes.' He grinned. 'You'll be safe with me.'

But my heart won't be, she thought as he disappeared into the cabin, and reappeared almost immediately, hand outstretched to lead her to the boat.

She felt a frisson as their fingers linked and then as he helped her in, settling her under the canopy and taking the wheel.

Maddie leaned back and closed her eyes, and as the boat chugged off in a very sedate manner she smiled, letting the wind blow her hair all round her face.

It was too noisy with the engine running to talk, and she liked that because she needed to think. She needed to do something with the churning in her head. She needed to sift through the tangle of confused thoughts and put them into some kind of order.

She needed to ask herself whether she had made the right decision in turning him down and whether it was too late to reverse that decision.

She half opened her eyes and drank him in. He'd unbuttoned his shirt and it whipped behind him, exposing the bronzed perfection of his torso. His swimming trunks were baggy, riding low on his lean hips, and he was steering with one hand, dark sunglasses in place.

He took her breath away.

He would take any woman's breath away.

If they were married, though, she wouldn't have to deal with the pain of watching him take those other women's breath away.

She walked towards him and stood right next to him, slinging her arm casually around his waist.

Leo stiffened, but didn't glance down at her.

'I'll anchor in a couple of minutes,' he said roughly. 'If you're not confident in the water you can stick to the side of the boat. The ladder will be down. You can climb up any time you get nervous. Or you don't have to come in at all. Although...' He breathed in the scent of her and felt a rush of desire. 'I hope you do. The water here is warm. If you're feeling brave, we can grab a couple of snorkels and see what's there.'

'Should I be scared?'

'Never with me around.'

He killed the engine and it spluttered into silence. When he drew back to look at her she was shading her eyes against the glare, her face upturned to his.

'You *do* make me feel safe,' she confided truthfully. 'And I know I haven't said this before, but I really appreciate everything you're doing for me now that I'm pregnant.'

Leo wondered whether she knew what that arm round his waist had done to him and how those glass-green eyes were affecting him.

'Good!' he said heartily. 'Swim?'

He turned away before his arousal became overpowering and paused on the edge of the boat, desperate for some cold water to kill his rampant libido.

'Definitely!' Maddie laughed and untied her sarong, and then faced him, still smiling.

She was the most beautiful thing he'd ever seen, and Leo dived into the sea before he let loose a groan of desire. He swam underwater, his powerful body sleek and brown as he sliced through the water and surfaced wiping his face.

She was tentatively taking the steps down and he swam towards her to help.

'I can manage!' Maddie laughed, but she did curve round and link her fingers behind his neck briefly before letting go and doggy-paddling by the ladder. 'This is as good as it gets with me. I can swim *a bit*…'

'Hang on to the ladder. I'm going to get the snorkels. There's a lifesaver ring you can hold, to make sure you don't feel out of your depth.'

'I won't need that,' Maddie teased breathlessly, 'Not when you're here and you've said that I can trust you.'

Hell, she was doing it again...turning him on when she obviously didn't mean to...

Five minutes later they were snorkelling, and Maddie was clearly having the time of her life.

It was strange that she'd never done anything like this before, especially as she'd lived in a country famed for its Great Barrier Reef and its exotic underwater life.

She got a bit braver the longer they were in the water, venturing further out holding on to Leo. She only reluctantly returned to the boat when he tapped her and told her how long they'd been swimming.

'That was amazing,' she confessed excitedly, removing the snorkel and shaking her hair, before flipping it into a makeshift braid that hung like a wet burnished gold rope down her back. 'I could do that every day!'

Leo grinned. 'Then we'll have to do something about that,' he drawled, towelling himself dry and slinging the damp towel across his shoulders.

Their eyes met and he didn't look away. Nor did she.

When she walked towards him—carefully, because a boat was not the steadiest surface in the world—he didn't move a muscle. He waited. As still and as watchful as a jungle animal on high alert.

He was picking up all sorts of signals and he didn't know what to believe and what not to believe. But when she stopped right in front of him and looked up at him he knew exactly what to believe.

'You shouldn't,' he said roughly.

'Shouldn't what?'

'Stand there looking at me as though you want me

to strip you bare and make love to you right here on this boat.'

Maddie looked down, suddenly shy. She was pregnant with his baby, and yet here she was *shy*?

'Is that what you want, *cara*?'

He tilted her chin and met her apple-green eyes steadily.

'Do you want me to do this?'

He trailed one long brown finger along her cleavage and she shuddered and let loose a stifled little gasp.

'What about this?'

He reached to the straps of her swimsuit and hooked his fingers under before he slowly began pulling them down, watching her carefully, getting more and more worked up with every passing second.

It was his turn to stifle a groan of pure pleasure as her breasts were exposed, pale orbs with those delectable rosy nipples, bigger and darker now, just as her breasts were fuller and heavier. He was startled to see that his hands were shaking as he rubbed the tips of her nipples with the pads of his thumbs. The swimsuit had bunched up at her waist and he badly wanted to take it off completely, but he hesitated.

'Is this what you want?' he demanded unsteadily. 'Because it's what *I* want…'

Maddie nodded, and Leo did what he wanted to do. He pulled off her swimsuit and then devoted himself to her body, tasting it, working his way down while she remained standing, holding on to the steel pole supporting the canopy. Her head was flung back and her mouth was half open as she moaned, a low, guttural sound as his mouth found the patch between her legs and he burrowed there, nuzzling before gently parting the folds of her womanhood so that he could slide his tongue into her slick groove.

Maddie plunged her fingers into his springy hair, arched her back and *enjoyed*. She opened her legs wider, sank against his tongue, bucked as it teased her and came explosively against his mouth, twisting and crying out while the sea breeze blew strands of hair across her open mouth and warmed her breasts.

'I can't stop wanting you,' she gasped, finally collapsing against him and letting him carry her down the stunted row of stairs that led to the small living area on the boat. There was no bed, but there was a long, upholstered bench seat, and he lay her down and stood up to look at her nakedness.

'And I you,' he growled.

Leo couldn't get his shirt off fast enough, and then the swimming trunks. And he couldn't take his eyes off her rosy flushed face. He was captivated by the way she lay there, idly stroking her breast with one hand, mesmerised by her swollen stomach.

'Is this safe?' he asked, sinking onto the bench seat alongside her and wishing he'd had the wit to install something more accommodating.

'Of course it is!' Maddie laughed and kissed him. 'I just need you, Leo. I need you to come inside me…'

Leo needed no further encouragement. Some foreplay? *Yes*. He suckled her breasts and idly played between her thighs. He wanted to devote more time to both, but he couldn't because his animal cravings were too intense.

This was his woman—ripe with his child. A surge of possessiveness and fierce pride rushed through him as he pushed into her, taking her in long, hard strokes, only just holding on for her to reach her peak before coming inside her, pouring himself into her and crying out with the pleasure and satisfaction of it.

He'd never experienced anything like it in his life before. He couldn't let this woman go. He couldn't let any other man hold the child she was carrying. The only man who would ever hold this baby would be him.

He was obviously a lot less New Age than he'd imagined.

'Marry me, Maddie.'

The silence was the length of a heartbeat and then Maddie nodded, still flushed from lovemaking.

'Okay.'

Leo dealt her a slow, slashing smile that took her breath away. 'You changed your mind?' he said, knowing he should leave well alone but needing to hear why she had come round to his way of thinking.

A post-coital rush of heated acquiescence would inevitably lead to a sober rethink in the cold light of day.

'I changed my mind,' Maddie said. 'In an ideal world, this isn't how I saw my life going—marrying a man for the sake of a baby. But it's not an ideal world and you were right. I should be the first to recognise that. I've seen how attentive you can be, Leo. You would make a great dad. That's enough for me.'

It would never really be enough, but it would have to do. And in time, who knew…? Perhaps he would come to love her the way she loved him.

'Are you sure?' His navy blue eyes were thoughtful. 'Sure you can do without the fairy tale? I'm not built for the business of falling in love, Maddie.'

Maddie didn't skip a beat, because she'd made her decision and she was going to stand by it. She adored this man, and she would always nurture the hope that his heart would open up to her, but she would never let him see that. He wanted a business transaction, and that was what he was going to get.

'I know,' she said, and shrugged. 'Maybe I'm not either. Now, let's not talk any more. Have I told you that I can't seem to get enough of you…?'

Maddie swept up the trail of clothes on the floor. On the bed, Leo was half dozing, half looking at her, sated after a bout of extremely satisfying early-morning sex.

'You're very untidy, Leo. Is that one of the bad habits of coming from a wealthy background? You're so used to people tidying up behind you that you've forgotten how to do it yourself?'

But her voice was light and teasing. The past three days had been the best three days of her entire life. He made her feel so safe, so secure, so *cherished*. Maddie knew that it was dangerous, but she could just *feel* something between them. He said he didn't 'do' love, but surely he wouldn't be so attentive and tender if he didn't feel at least *some* of what she was feeling. Surely!

He had never spoken about what had turned him off all the things that propelled most normal people into marriage, for better or for worse, and she hadn't asked. They had their pact and she wasn't going to start rocking any boats. She was going to play the long game.

She picked up his shorts, tutting, and shook them, dislodging his wallet from the pocket. It flew open, discharging its contents. Platinum cards, business cards, cash and…

Maddie frowned and stooped to retrieve the picture

that had fallen out along with everything else. She held it up to the light.

Staring back at her was a fair-haired woman with full lips and bright blue laughing eyes. There was something knowing about those eyes. And an undeniable sensuality. The woman was looking down at whoever was taking the picture and her lips were parted...teasing, tempting.

Maddie shivered—because now she *knew*. She walked over to Leo, who had sat up, and showed him the picture.

'Who's this?' she asked lightly.

Leo stilled. He reached for the photo without bothering to look at it and stuck it on the bedside table.

She'd hoped he would say it was no one of any importance, but a steely resolve had washed over his features when he turned back to her.

'That is my ex-wife.'

CHAPTER TEN

'YOUR EX-*WIFE*,' MADDIE said woodenly, folding her arms, colour draining from her face faster than water going down a drain. 'You were *married*. And you didn't think that it was important enough to tell me?'

Suddenly restless, Leo vaulted upright, gloriously and unashamedly naked. He grabbed the nearest item of clothing, which happened to be his boxers, and stepped into them.

'How is it something that impacts on us?' His voice was cool and toneless, and that said more than words alone could ever say.

That woman in the picture was his wife, who had meant so much to him that he couldn't even let her name pass his lips. *This* was the mysterious reason why he wasn't interested in love. Because he'd been there before. He'd given his heart to someone else and he no longer possessed one to give to anyone who followed.

All Maddie's dreams and hopes about time working its magic and building the sort of love in him for her that she felt for him had been castles in the sand, now washed away by grim reality.

'"How is it something that impacts on us?"'

Maddie stared at him with incredulity and Leo had the grace to flush.

'It's in the past.'

'But don't you think it's a past you should have *told* me about? I mean, you know all about mine…'

'You chose to tell me,' Leo pointed out, with the sort of remorseless logic that set her teeth on edge. Caught on the back foot, Leo always fell back on his automatic instinct to defend himself.

'I chose to *share* my past with you.'

'The implication being that I should return the favour?'

'Most normal people would.'

'Haven't you deduced by now that I don't play by the same rules?'

Yes, Maddie thought miserably, yes, she had. She had just opted to ignore it.

She flung on her dressing gown and stared down at her bare feet, at the pale pink of the polish she had put on her toenails the evening before.

'Where is she now?' she asked stiffly, wondering if she should be on the lookout for the sexy blonde he had loved popping out from the nearest wardrobe or lurking behind the bushes wearing nothing but that sexy, *sexy* smile.

'Things didn't work out.'

'"Things didn't work out"? But you still keep a picture of her in your wallet?'

What sort of response *was that*? What did *things didn't work out* even *mean*? Obviously whatever had happened he had been bitterly hurt and fatally scarred.

'Where are you going with this, Maddie? That part of my past has nothing to do with us. You have to trust me.'

Maddie swallowed back her hurt. She had agreed to marry this man and she loved him. He had his past, just as she had hers, and marrying him would mean living with that and dealing with it, but she couldn't live without him.

She knew what would happen if she got into a flaming row with him over this. He would vanish. To his office or out in the Jeep to a beach, or into the garden... Anywhere just as long as she wasn't there, because he wasn't going to deal with her hysterics.

Dealing with her hysterics and her jealousy wasn't part of their business transaction.

'I'm going to have a bath,' she said, turning away.

Leo nodded and said nothing. What was there to say? He had closed the door on that slice of his past and he wasn't going to re-open it. What would be the good in that? Maddie would have to trust him.

But he had glimpsed that shattered expression on her face as she had turned away and something inside him had twisted painfully.

He didn't wait for her to emerge. Instead he flung on some clothes, headed down to the pool and washed away his restlessness by swimming lap after lap after lap until every muscle in his body was aching.

When he returned to the villa it was to find her in the kitchen, seemingly back to normal.

'Where were you?' she asked from where she was standing by the stove, putting on a saucepan with some butter, ready for the eggs that stood on the counter nearby.

It must have taken so much for her to act as though nothing had happened, but she managed it.

She also managed to smile at him.

'I'm making us some of those eggs we bought at the market this morning.'

Leo looked at her, trying to gauge her mood and feeling a little disconcerted that there was nothing to gauge. If she'd been hurt by his silence then she'd recovered fast. He frowned, not knowing how that speedy recovery made him feel.

'Okay. Great. I was in the pool.'

He hovered, for once indecisive. Should he revive the subject of Claire? He frowned, because it wasn't like him to backtrack on any decision once that decision had been made—and he'd made the decision not to start babbling on about his past, on which the door had been shut.

'It looks lovely out there,' Maddie said gaily, a broad smile pinned to her face.

She sounded like a Stepford Wife. All that was missing was the gingham apron.

'Anyway, breakfast will be ready in about five minutes. Does that give you enough time to change?'

Leo grunted and disappeared, duly reappearing in under five minutes in a pair of faded blue Bermuda shorts and a white tee shirt, barefoot as always. He couldn't see the point of wearing shoes in the villa when the floor was so warm.

He gritted his teeth and wondered how it was that he was about to bring up a subject he had only minutes before sworn to avoid.

'About Claire…'

Maddie looked at him seriously. Really? He wanted to talk about his ex? Did he think that she actually *wanted* to hear about how much he had given himself to a relationship that hadn't worked out? Did she need an explanation as to why he could never give again?

No way. That would not only be a dagger to her heart, but a dagger twisting and swivelling and causing maximum damage. *Thanks, but no thanks.*

'No,' she said.

'No?'

'I don't want to talk about her. Like you said, that's your past and this is the present. We both know why we're going into this…er…arrangement. We both know that it's not the sort of marriage that most people dream about. But it's the right thing for us to do. I know that. Like I said, I've seen for myself what a good dad you would make, and we might not be a traditional couple, with all the traditional hopes and dreams, but we get along all right and that's the main thing.'

Said out loud, it sounded like a poor excuse for a union. But then she thought of her life without Leo, and the horror that image conjured up reaffirmed why she was doing what she was. He would never love her. He hadn't been lying when he'd said that he just didn't have it in him. But she would always love *him*.

She was surprised to see that Leo didn't look relieved and elated that they were on the same page. The look on his face was more…*dissatisfaction*.

He swept aside her response. 'We have something else going for us.'

'What's that?'

'This.'

He pulled her towards him and kissed her. Kissed her until she was drugged with wanting him and on fire to have him touch her the way only he could.

When he did this—kissed her and held her and let

his body do the talking—she forgot everything. Forgot the fact that she was in love with a man who'd given his heart away to someone else. Forgot that she felt like a hypocrite, hiding her aching heart under a cheery smile.

She grunted with pleasure as he pushed down her shorts so that he could caress her swollen belly.

Her pregnancy fascinated him, and his fascination thrilled her. He slid his fingers lower, taking his time to caress her intimately with slow, rhythmic movements that left her panting with pleasure.

He whispered in her ear what he wanted to do to her, where he wanted to touch and feel and taste, until Maddie was giddy with desire. Then, still taking his time, he sat her on the edge of the table and she supported herself, hands stretched out behind her, palms flat on the smooth, polished wood.

He tugged off the shorts, taking her knickers at the same time, and pushed up her tee shirt so that he could see her breasts. Then he undid his zipper and dropped his shorts to the ground.

Her eyes were closed and she sighed and moaned softly as he slid into her, angling her body so that he could take her in a few thrusts. Quick, hot sex that swept away everything in its path.

'I can't get enough of you…' he growled, when they were both sated and normal business had resumed—although the eggs were burned and had had to be chucked.

Enough of the sex, Maddie completed in her head. But she couldn't get enough of that either. And that, if she was going through the *pros* checklist, counted for a lot.

'Well, you'll have to make do for the moment,' she told him lightly. 'We've made plans for today. I'm looking forward to seeing that cove you were telling me about.'

Another bright smile. Her jaw was beginning to ache from the effort of those bright smiles.

Leo kissed the tip of her nose.

'And then back to Dublin,' Maddie said, tidying up, thinking of the house she'd left behind, which she knew was now in great order because Leo had been showing her daily updates of the work that was being done. Only the attic needed a bit of sprucing up.

'But not like before,' Leo reminded her. 'This time back to Dublin as a couple.'

Maddie choked down a painful lump. 'Yes,' she mumbled, looking away, 'as a couple…'

It was another two and a half weeks before Maddie finally made it up to the attic—the final thing on her to-do list. With Leo's support, everything that had seemed difficult and daunting had become manageable. He had helped in ways that he had said were small and incidental, but when she examined them later she saw they were huge and fundamental.

The house was near completion and new staff had been hired at the store and renovations had begun. The cobwebby elegance of a past era was being replaced by a modernist vision, but it was going to stay as the store it was meant to be.

The attic was her final as yet unexplored territory, which was why now, at a little after six in the evening, with Leo due to come over in an hour, Maddie was sitting on the ground surrounded by…*stuff.*

Boxes of old bills, receipts, random scraps of paper with names on them, which she deciphered as being the names of horses or dogs or whatever it was her grand-father had been wont to bet on. And then there were the pictures. These Maddie took her time with, look-ing at them one by one. Pictures of her grandmother, her mother—photos dating back decades.

She was barely aware of Leo, padding up the wind-ing narrow staircase that led off from one of the top bedrooms to the enormous attic.

'You can help,' she announced, pausing to look at him and then struggling to tear her eyes away, as al-ways happened.

He'd come straight from work. He'd already located premises for his offices, and magically everything had been completed with supersonic speed. His faith in the power of money had not been misplaced.

'Okay. I'll arrange for a clearance company. They can come in and remove the entire lot. I've never been in such an unmitigated disaster zone in my entire life.'

'I've got some photos here, Leo.' She shuffled over to where he had taken up residence on the floor and sat next to him, going through the pictures, marvelling at the past unfolding in front of her. Her mother had been quite remarkable-looking—as had her grandparents.

'He went bad after your grandmother died,' Leo said neutrally.

'Your grandfather told you that?'

'There was bad blood between them before that, with the acquisition of the store premises, but I believe there was some scattered correspondence between them for a while after. When your grandmother died the old man went down a different road.'

'You've not mentioned any of that before,' Maddie murmured absently, sifting through the photos and at the bottom finding a slender stack of envelopes. Maybe five.

Her mother's handwriting was on them, and Leo reached out to take them from her.

'Maddie…'

But she was already opening the first letter and Leo's jaw clenched as he read it over her shoulder—read the pleading note from Lizzie Gallo to her unforgiving father, and knew that the other letters would be along the same lines.

'Leo…' Maddie whispered, turning to look at him. 'I thought…'

'You did,' Leo said gravely.

He stroked her hair away from her face, noted the way her eyes had glazed over, the quiver of her mouth. If the old bastard had been around he wouldn't have seen the light of another day.

'You knew?'

He nodded on a sigh. 'Yes,' he confessed. 'There were words between Tommaso and my grandfather a long time ago. Probably shortly after your mother had decamped to Australia. Who knows whether she did that to get away from the toxic atmosphere in the house? Tommaso never recovered from Susan's death. My grandfather got in touch about buying the store. He got a letter back. I won't bother to tell you what it said. I imagine you can guess the gist.'

'That he would never sell the store—just like he would never forgive my mother, even though she'd begged for forgiveness. She had it so hard in Australia. Worked her fingers to the bone to earn money for both of us. And he refused to give her anything.'

'He was a bastard.'

'You never said…'

'You had your dreams and I wasn't going to shatter them,' Leo told her.

'I don't want the store,' Maddie whispered. 'It was never a legacy of love.'

'You don't know that.' Leo sighed. 'Things change when you're facing the grim reaper. Who knows what was going through the old man's head when he made that will?'

'You think?'

'I do think. Your mother was stubborn, and so was he. He couldn't bring himself to forgive, but he must have lived a life of regret—hence the gambling and the alcohol.'

'Why didn't you say anything?'

'I couldn't hurt you, Maddie.' He drew his breath in. 'I could never hurt you,' he continued in a roughened undertone.

He shifted so that he was looking directly at her. The lighting in the attic was dim—just shafts of watery sunshine filtering through the glass of the four Velux windows on the slanting roof.

'I need to tell you about my ex-wife. About Claire.'

'Please don't, Leo. I… I… No, please don't. I understand how you feel. Things didn't work out and it hurt you so much that you still can't bear to talk about it. You loved and you lost and, lest you forget, you keep her photo in your wallet. I get it. I just don't want the details.' She smiled weakly. 'There's such a thing as too much information.'

'Silly fool,' Leo said tenderly. 'Is that what you think?'

'What else? No one hangs on to a photo of someone they couldn't give a hoot about.'

'I keep that photo as a reminder of the biggest mistake I ever made,' he said heavily, and Maddie's eyebrows shot up in surprise. 'I was young and cocky and I fell for an older woman.' He grinned crookedly. 'I was a cliché, in other words. Except I was rich, so I could *get* the older woman. But she turned out to be a fortune-hunter who had spotted in me the perfect opportunity to feather her nest. And, rich young buck that I was, I fell for it hook, line and sinker. I married her and it lasted about two seconds. It was the most expensive mistake I ever made. She took the money and vanished as a wealthy divorcee, and after that...'

'You threw away the key to your heart?'

Maddie wanted to keep grounded, but inside she was taking flight, heady with the realisation that her assumptions had been unfounded.

'I threw away the key to my heart,' Leo concurred. 'And I thought that it was for the best. No love and no pretending that I was capable of it. I never banked on *you* coming along.'

'Say that again?' Maddie held her breath and tried hard to look puzzled and yet empathetic when inside her heart was racing and her mouth was dry.

'I never banked on you coming along. I never banked on falling in love. *Really* in love. In love so that I can't think of life without you in it, Maddie. In love so that if anyone tries to hurt you, I will kill them.'

'Leo...' Slowly, she smiled, heady and deliriously happy. 'You're saying all the right things.'

She reached out and ran a dusty finger across his cheek.

'I love you so much. I knew that you wanted a pragmatic relationship, and I knew that was the last thing

I wanted, but I also knew that I would rather have that with you than have anything else with anybody else. I never thought I would fall in love with you—not after everything I'd been through—but I did. Bit by bit I came to see you for the wonderful man you are. Thoughtful, kind, considerate, funny...'

'Scintillating...sexy...'

'Egotistical...untidy...terrible at cooking... The memory of that steak you cooked for me last week will live on in my head for ever...'

'Hey! That last one's going too far!' Leo burst out laughing. When he'd sobered up, he said, seriously, 'I would get down on one knee, Maddie, but I'm already sitting. Will you marry me? For the *right* reasons? Because I love you and need you and can't live without you?'

'Just try and stop me!'

Maddie flung her arms round his neck. She was living her own fairy tale. Whoever said that they couldn't come true?

The wedding was low-key. They both wanted to exchange vows before the baby was born, so less than three months later a very pregnant Maddie walked up the aisle in a picturesque church on the outskirts of Dublin.

Leo's grandfather, beaming with pride, was in attendance, accompanied by a female friend whom, he confided to Maddie, he had been seeing 'off and on' for over a year and a half.

'I've never mentioned it to Leo,' he said, 'because I'm an old fool, and you know how matter-of-fact that grandson of mine can be. Didn't want him pooh-poohing the whole thing. But all that's changed, thanks to you, my dear. The minute I met you I knew that you were the one who was going to change him for the better. No, maybe *better* isn't the word I'm looking for—because no one could ever accuse Leo of being anything but an honourable man. Maybe change him for the *softer*, if that makes any sense.'

Maddie didn't tell him that there hadn't been that much to change after all, because there had been a softie buried deep down all the time.

By now she had made friends in Dublin. Other mums-to-be, several members of staff at the store, who were all now energised as the store finally began to pay dividends.

It had been a two-pronged effort—one that had been shared between her and Leo. She had listened to his ideas for introducing a dedicated electronics department, which was loosely based on his original idea for what he had intended to do with the store, but scaled down considerably. In time, he would source a suitable location and expand operations there. He had given way to her with the rest. She had laughed when he'd suggested lending a hand when it came to choosing sexy lingerie for the women's department.

'It would definitely work,' he had murmured one evening, when they'd both been warm and sated and wrapped round one another in bed after some very satisfying lovemaking, 'if you try on each sample piece for me to inspect...'

The store had brought them together and now, for Maddie, it was something special—something more than just concrete and stone—and it would be for ever. She quietly hoped, and so did Leo, that it would be a legacy they would be able to pass down to their children, and their children's children, that its story would be told over and over until it became the backdrop to their lives. A very happy and wonderful story, despite its inauspicious beginnings.

There were no relatives for her at the small wedding—no brothers or sisters or aunts or uncles—but Maddie didn't mind. She had the most important person in the world there. She was marrying the man who had spotted her once upon a time in a store she had been battling to hang on to, and the rest, as he fondly told her, was history.

After the wedding they went on a flying honeymoon to a five-star hotel in Cornwall, and they had a wonderful time in driving rain and under heavy grey skies, wrapped up in woollens, as happy holding hands there as if they'd been on the most expensive trip to the Maldives.

'When the baby comes and you can travel comfortably,' Leo promised, 'we're going to go sailing down the Grenadines. Until then…' he looked up at the leaden skies and grinned '…we're going to enjoy the wonderful English countryside in typical English weather. It'll stand me in good stead for when we move out to the country.'

Having done up her grandfather's house to the highest possible standard, Maddie found herself reluctant to live there.

'I can forgive my grandfather for the sin of pride,' she'd admitted, 'but I can't forget. And I'll always wonder what life would have been like for me and Mum if he'd just relented and forgiven her for running away.'

'Too arrogant and too stubborn,' Leo had murmured.

'Those were traits he had even as a young man, according to my grandfather, and they probably became out of control the older he got and the lonelier he became. And don't forget he was gambling and drinking heavily. Those two things would have turned his brain to mush and wreaked havoc on his ability to think clearly.'

So they'd found a lovely little house, close to the very church where they'd married. And, of course, there was Leo's London place, which was every bit as luxurious as she remembered. But Dublin, he confessed, had grown on him.

Flora Madison Conti was born three days after her due date with no fuss at all.

Dark-haired and green-eyed, she was sweet-natured and, within hours of coming into the world, already the apple of her father's eye.

Their real honeymoon, taken when Flora was a little over three months old, was as perfect as anything Maddie could have hoped for, and made all the better when she received news that the store, for the first time in over a decade, had shown a profit.

Maddie thought that if only her mother could have seen her she would have been bursting with pride that her daughter had married for love—and also highly amused that Maddie was now in charge of the very store from which she had once been exiled.

Now, with Flora asleep, Maddie was in the kitchen in their beautiful little house, with her very domesticated alpha male husband due back at any second.

She heard the key in the lock and the sound of the door opening and her heart skipped a beat. Leo never failed to command her attention.

He strode in and smiled as his dark eyes rested on

her. Sitting there, with her long toffee-coloured hair swept over one shoulder and her golden skin glowing, she was the very picture of everything any man could ever hope for.

He was lucky, and he knew that he was. He had resigned himself to a life without love and he couldn't believe how naïve he had been in thinking that he could ever have been happy in a union that was devoid of it.

'Flora asleep, my darling?'

'She is…' Maddie stood up and walked towards him, and with every step closer her pulse raced faster and her pupils dilated. She felt the push of her breasts against her bra. 'And I've cooked us something special.'

'Tell me I haven't forgotten a special day… The anniversary of the first time you thought I was a wandering explorer…? Or maybe of the first time you realised that you were head over heels in love with the only man you'll ever need…?'

He grinned and pulled her to him, kissed her with lingering thoroughness.

'Sweet,' he murmured. 'Like nectar. Now, this special meal…will it wait?'

'Leo…!'

But Maddie giggled and tingled as he unhooked her bra and cupped her breast in his hand as though weighing it.

'Is that a plea for sex? Because if it is, then your wish is my command.'

'Is that *all* you think about?'

'It's all I've been thinking about since about…oh… three this afternoon. Highly inappropriate, given that I was in a high-level meeting at the time.' He stood back and looked at her, his beautiful eyes tender and serious.

'But I think about other things too. I think about how much I love being married to you and how bloody happy you make me. I think about how much I'm looking forward to growing old with you and sharing my life with you. And I think about my stunning little baby girl.'

'That's a lot of thinking for a top businessman like you,' Maddie said, and laughed.

'And that's not all I've been thinking about…' Leo murmured as they headed up the stairs to their bedroom suite, which was next to the nursery where Flora was fast asleep.

'No?' She was breathless as they entered the bedroom and he quietly shut the door behind them, not bothering to switch on the lights.

She began undoing the buttons of his shirt until it was open, and then she rubbed his flat brown nipple with the pad of her thumb, making him shudder at the delicate touch. When she rested her hand on the bulging erection pushing against his trousers, he stifled a moan.

'Tell me what else you've been thinking about…' She guided his hand to her loose skirt and then encouraged him to explore further, to touch her under the floaty fabric, through her lacy underwear, to feel her wetness on his fingers.

'You mean aside from what you want me to do to you right now?'

On cue, he slipped his big hand under her knickers and began rubbing between her legs with the flat of his hand. He wasn't in any rush to take things faster just yet. He kept on rubbing, before slipping a finger deep into her, loving the way her muscles contracted at the intimate contact.

'Keep that up and I won't remember what it is we're talking about,' Maddie panted unevenly.

'Okay…' Leo slid his finger to find the nub of her core and transferred his attention there. 'Here's what I've been thinking. What about making another baby, my darling? Right now?'

Maddie giggled and sighed and looked at him from under her lashes, her whole body on fire as he continued to devastate her senses with his finger.

'And that's why I adore you,' she breathed. 'You can read my mind…'

* * * * *

COMING SOON!

We really hope you enjoyed reading this book. If you're looking for more romance, be sure to head to the shops when new books are available on

Thursday
9th August

To see which titles are coming soon, please visit
millsandboon.co.uk

MILLS & BOON

Coming next month

THE HEIR THE PRINCE SECURES
Jennie Lucas

He eyed the baby in the stroller, who looked back at him with dark eyes exactly like his own. He said simply, 'I need you and Esme with me.'

'In London?'

Leaning forward, he whispered, 'Everywhere.'

She felt the warmth of his breath against her skin, and her heartbeat quickened. For so long, Tess would have done anything to hear Stefano speak those words.

But she'd suffered too much shock and grief today. He couldn't tempt her to forget so easily how badly he'd treated her. She pulled away.

'Why would I come with you?'

Stefano's eyes widened. She saw she'd surprised him.

Giving her a crooked grin, he said, 'I can think of a few reasons.'

'If you want to spend time with Esme, I will be happy to arrange that. But if you think I'll give up my family and friends and home—' she lifted her chin '—and come with you to Europe as some kind of paid nanny—'

'No. Not my nanny.' Stefano's thumb lightly traced her tender lower lip. 'I have something else in mind.'

Unwilling desire shot down her body, making her nipples taut as tension coiled low in her belly. Her pride was screaming for her to push him away but it was difficult to hear her pride over the rising pleas of her body.

'I—I won't be your mistress, either,' she stammered, shivering, searching his gaze.

'No.' With a smile that made his dark eyes gleam, Stefano shook his head. 'Not my mistress.'

'Then…then what?' Tess stammered, feeling foolish for even suggesting a handsome billionaire prince like Stefano would want a regular girl like her as his mistress. Her cheeks were hot. 'You don't want me as your nanny, not as your mistress, so—what? You just want me to come to London as someone who watches your baby for free?' Her voice shook. 'Some kind of…p-poor relation?'

'No.' Taking her in his arms, Stefano said quietly, 'Tess. Look at me.'

Although she didn't want to obey, she could not resist. She opened her eyes, and the intensity of his glittering eyes scared her.

'I don't want you to be my mistress, Tess. I don't want you to be my nanny.' His dark eyes burned through her. 'I want you to be my wife.'

Continue reading
THE HEIR THE PRINCE SECURES
Jennie Lucas

Available next month
www.millsandboon.co.uk

LET'S TALK
Romance

For exclusive extracts, competitions
and special offers, find us online:

f facebook.com/millsandboon

◯ @millsandboonuk

𝕏 @millsandboon

Or get in touch on 0844 844 1351*

For all the latest titles coming soon, visit
millsandboon.co.uk/nextmonth